Katie,
batter
up!

This book is a work of fiction. Any references to historical events, real people, or real places are used fictitiously. Other names, characters, places, and events are products of the author's imagination, and any resemblance to actual events or places or persons, living or dead, is entirely coincidental.

SIMON SPOTLIGHT
An imprint of Simon & Schuster Children's Publishing Division
1230 Avenue of the Americas, New York, New York 10020
Copyright © 2011 by Simon & Schuster, Inc.
All rights reserved, including the right of reproduction
in whole or in part in any form.
SIMON SPOTLIGHT and colophon are registered
trademarks of Simon & Schuster, Inc.
Text by Tracey West
Chapter header illustrations by Laura Roode
Design by Laura Roode
For information about special discounts for bulk purchases, please contact
Simon & Schuster Special Sales
at 1-866-506-1949 or business@simonandschuster.com.
Manufactured in the United States of America 0713 FFG
First Edition
2 4 6 8 10 9 7 5 3 1
ISBN 978-4424-8564-8 (hc)
ISBN 978-1-4424-4611-3 (pbk)
ISBN 978-1-4424-4612-0 (eBook)
Library of Congress Control Number 2011940765

CUPCAKE DIARIES

Katie, batter up!

by coco simon

Simon Spotlight

New York   London   Toronto   Sydney   New Delhi

CHAPTER 1

My Cupcake Obsession

My name is Katie Brown, and I am crazy about cupcakes. I'm not kidding. I think about cupcakes every day. I even dream about them when I sleep. The other night I was dreaming that I was eating a giant cupcake, and when I woke up I was chewing on my pillow!

Okay, now I *am* kidding. But I do dream about cupcakes, I swear. There must be a name for this condition. Cupcake-itis? That's got to be it. I am stricken with cupcake-itis, and there isn't any cure.

My three best friends and I formed the Cupcake Club, and we bake cupcakes for parties and events and things, and sell them. We're all different in our own way. Mia has long black hair and loves fashion. Emma has blond hair and blue eyes and lots of brothers. Alexis has wavy red hair and loves math.

I have light brown hair, and I mostly wear jeans and T-shirts. I'm an only child. And I hate math. But I have one big thing in common with all my friends: We love cupcakes.

That's why we were in my kitchen on a Tuesday afternoon, baking cupcakes on a beautiful spring day. We were having an official meeting to discuss our next big job: baking a cupcake cake for my grandma Carole's seventy-fifth birthday bash. But while we were thinking about that, we were also trying to perfect a new chocolate-coconut-almond cupcake, specially created for my friend Mia's stepdad and based on his favorite candy bar.

We had tried two different combinations already: a chocolate cupcake with coconut frosting and almonds on top and then a coconut cupcake with chocolate-almond frosting, but none of them matched the taste of the candy bar enough. Now we were working on a third batch: a chocolate-almond cupcake with coconut frosting and lots of shredded coconut on top.

I carefully poured a teaspoon of almond extract into the batter. "Mmm, smells almondy," I said.

"I hope this batch is the one," said Mia. "Eddie finally started taking down that gross flowery wallpaper in my bedroom, and I have to find some way to thank him. I would have paid someone a million dollars to do that!"

"You realize you could buy a whole new house for a million dollars, right?" Alexis asked. "Probably two or three."

"You know what I mean," Mia replied. "Besides, you know how ugly that wallpaper is. It looks like something you'd find in an old lady's room."

"Hey, my grandma Carole's an old lady, and she doesn't have ugly wallpaper in *her* house," I protested.

Emma picked up the ice-cream scoop and started scooping up the batter and putting it into the cupcake pans.

"We need to find out more about your grandma," Emma said. "That way we can figure out what kind of cupcake cake to make for the party."

"Right!" Alexis agreed. She flipped open her notebook and took out the pen that was tucked behind her ear. Sometimes I think Alexis must have a secret stash of notebooks in her house somewhere. I've never seen her without one.

"First things first," Alexis said. "How many people are coming to the party?"

I wrinkled my nose, thinking. "Not sure," I said.

Then I yelled as loud as I could. "Mom! How many people are coming to Grandma Carole's party?"

My mom appeared in the kitchen doorway. "Katie, you know how I feel about yelling," she said.

"Sorry, Mom," I said in my best apology voice.

"The answer is about thirty people," Mom said. "So I think if the cupcake cake has three dozen cupcakes, that would be fine."

"What exactly is a cupcake cake, anyway?" Mia asked. "Do you mean like one of those giant cupcakes that you bake with a special pan?"

"I was thinking more like a bunch of cupcakes arranged in tiers to look like a cake," Mom replied.

Mia nodded to Alexis's pen and notebook. "Can I?"

"Sure," Alexis replied, handing them to her. Mia began to sketch. She's a great artist and wants to be a fashion designer someday.

"Like this?" Mia asked, showing Mom the drawing. I looked over Mia's shoulder and saw the plan: three round tiers, one on top of the other, with cupcakes on each.

"Exactly!" Mom said, smiling and showing off a mouth full of perfect white teeth. (She *is* a dentist, after all.)

Alexis took back her notebook. "Excellent," she said, jotting something down. "Now we just need to decide what flavor to make and how to decorate it."

"What do you think, Mom?" I asked.

"Oh, I'm staying out of this. This is your project," Mom replied. "I think I'll let you girls come up with something. You always come up with such wonderful ideas, and I know Grandma Carole will love whatever you do."

"All done!" Emma announced, putting down the ice-cream scoop.

"Mom, oven, please?" I asked.

"Sure thing," Mom said, slipping on an oven mitt. She put the chocolate-almond cupcakes into the preheated oven, and I set the cupcake-shaped timer on the counter for twenty minutes.

Mom left the kitchen, and the four of us sat down at the kitchen table to work out the details.

"So what kind of flavors does your grandmother like?" Alexis asked.

I shrugged. "I don't know. She likes all kinds of things. Blueberry pie in the summer, and chocolate cake, and maple-walnut ice cream . . ."

"So we can make blueberry-chocolate-maple cupcakes with walnuts on top!" Mia joked.

"Hey, we thought bacon flavor was weird and that worked out well!" said Emma. It was true. Bacon flavor was a really big seller for us.

"You know, we don't know anything about your grandma," Emma said. "Maybe if you tell us something about her, we can get some ideas."

"Sure," I said. "Hold on a minute."

I went into the den where Mom and I keep all our books and picked up a photo album. We have lots of them, and there were pictures of Grandma Carole in almost all of them. I turned to a photo of me and my mom with Grandma Carole and Grandpa Chuck at Christmas. Grandma Carole looked nice in a red sweater and the beaded necklace I made her as a present at camp. Her hair used to be brown like mine, but now it's white.

"That's her," I said. "And that's my grandpa Chuck. They got married, like, forever ago, and they have three kids: my mom and my uncle Mike and my uncle Jimmy. She used to be a librarian."

"Just like my mom!" Emma said, smiling.

I flipped the pages in the photo album and found a picture of Grandma Carole in her white tennis outfit, holding her racquet.

6

"Mostly she loves sports and stuff," I said. "She runs, like, every day, and she won track medals in high school. She goes swimming and plays tennis, and skis in the winter, and she likes golf even though she says there's not enough running."

"Do sports have a flavor?" Mia mused.

"Um, sports-drink-flavored cupcakes?" Alexis offered.

"Or sweat-flavored cupcakes," I said, then burst out giggling.

"Or smelly sneaker-flavored cupcakes," Mia said, laughing.

"Ew, sweat and sneakers . . . those are so gross!" Emma squealed.

"But I guess she does like sports most of all," I said. "She's always trying to get me to do stuff with her. Because I am *soooo* good at sports." I said that really sarcastically, because the exact opposite is true. Now it was Emma's turn to giggle.

"Yeah, I've seen you in gym," she said.

"It's even worse than you know," I confessed. "When she tried to teach me to ski, I wiped out on the bunny hill—you know, the one for little kids? I even sprained my ankle."

"Oh, that's terrible!" Emma cried.

"And when I played tennis on a team with

Grandpa, I accidentally whacked him in the head with my racquet."

Mia put a hand to her mouth to try to stop from laughing. "Oh, Katie, that would be funny if it weren't so terrible!" she said.

I nodded. "He needed four stitches."

"So I guess you don't take after your grandmother," Alexis said.

"Well, not the sports thing," I admitted. "But everyone says I look exactly like she did when she was younger. And she's a good baker, too. She used to own her own cake baking business."

Alexis stood up. "You're kidding! Why didn't you tell us?"

"I just did," I said.

"But she's a *professional*," Alexis said. "It's not going to be easy to impress her."

"Yes, the pressure is on," Mia agreed.

I hadn't thought of that before. "Well, we'll just have to make a superawesome cupcake cake, then."

Alexis sat back down. "Okay, people, let's start jotting down some ideas."

We tried for the next few minutes, but nobody could think of anything. Then Emma looked at her watch.

"You know, I need to get home," she said. "It's my turn to make dinner tonight."

"We need some more time to come up with ideas, anyway," Alexis said. "Let's schedule another meeting."

"Let's do it tomorrow," I suggested. But Alexis and Mia had whipped out their smartphones, and Emma took out a little notebook with flowers on it—and they were all frowning.

"Alexis and I have soccer practice tomorrow and Thursday, and a game on Friday," Mia reported.

"And I have concert band practice on Wednesdays and Fridays," Emma said. Emma plays the flute, and she's really good at that.

"Sorry, Katie. You know spring is a busy time of year," Alexis said.

"Yeah, sure," I said, but really, I didn't. I don't really do anything besides the Cupcake Club, and it's not just because I have cupcake-itis. I'm no good at sports, and I'm not so great at music, either. When we learned how to play the recorder in fourth grade, I ended up making a sound like a beached whale. My teacher made me practice after school, after everyone went home.

Just then the cake timer rang. I put on a mitt and opened the oven door. All the cupcakes in the pan were flat. They should have gotten nice and puffy as they cooked.

"Mom!" I yelled.

Mom rushed in a few seconds later. "Katie, what did I tell you about—Oh," she said, looking at the deflated cupcakes.

"What happened?" I asked.

"This looks like a baking powder issue to me," she said. She put the pan of flat cupcakes on the counter and picked up the little can of baking powder. "Just as I thought. It's past its expiration date. You need fresh baking powder for your cupcakes to rise."

I felt terrible. "Sorry, guys."

"It's not your fault," Emma said.

"Yeah, and anyway, Eddie's not finished taking down that wallpaper yet," Mia said. "We can try again next time."

"Whenever that is," I mumbled.

Emma, Alexis, and Mia started picking up their things.

"We can talk about your grandma's cupcakes at lunch on Friday," Alexis said. "Everybody come with some ideas, okay?"

Emma saluted. "Yes, General Alexis!" she teased.

"Ooh, if Alexis is the general, can I be the cupcake captain?" I asked, and everyone laughed.

When my friends left, the kitchen was pretty quiet. Mom went into the den to do some paper-work, and all that was left was me and a pan of flat cupcakes.

As I cleaned up the mess, I thought of Alexis and Mia and Emma all going off and doing stuff—stuff that I couldn't do. They were all multitalented, and the only thing I was good at was making cupcakes. It made me feel a little bit lonely and a little bit like a loser.

In fact, it made me feel as flat as those cupcakes.

Yummy!

CHAPTER 2

Do I Really Look Like a Deer?

After I cleaned up I did my math homework while Mom made dinner, but that did not exactly improve my mood. In fact, when I sat down to eat I was feeling flatter than ever, even though Mom made tofu and broccoli in sesame sauce, which is superdelicious. (And please don't go hating on tofu. It's got a bad rap, but that stuff is pretty tasty. You should try it sometime.)

But that night even the deliciousness of tofu couldn't get me out of my mood. Mom noticed right away. She always does. I think it's because it's just the two of us in the house most of the time. Dad left when I was little, and I don't have any brothers or sisters, like I said before. If I had a big family, like Emma's, I could probably sulk through dinner without being spotted. But Mom started with the questions right away.

"What's wrong, Katie? Did you get enough sleep last night? You weren't up reading under the covers again, were you?"

"No, Mom, I'm not sleepy," I said.

"Are you feeling sick? Does your throat hurt?"

"No," I said, picking at some tofu with my fork. I didn't look up from the plate.

Then Mom changed her tone. Her voice got softer. "Okay, honey. If there's something you want to talk about, I'm here."

That understanding mom voice always gets me, even when I don't feel like talking. I put down my fork.

"It's kind of hard to explain," I said. "It's just . . . Mia and Alexis and Emma all do other stuff besides the Cupcake Club. Like play soccer and flute, and Emma walks dogs . . . and I don't do anything. Besides the Cupcake Club, I mean."

Mom didn't say anything right away. Then she said, "Well, you do well in school, and the Cupcake Club takes up a lot of your time. But maybe doing a different kind of activity isn't a bad idea. Is there something you're interested in?"

"That's the problem," I said. "I'm not good at

sports. I'm just not. I'm the worst in my whole gym class. And I could never play an instrument like Emma. Remember what happened when I learned the recorder?"

Mom cringed. "Oh dear. I see what you mean," she said. "But sports and music aren't the only things the school offers. I'll tell you what. After dinner let's get on the computer and look at the school website. Okay?"

"Okay," I agreed. It actually sounded like a good idea. Why hadn't I thought of that before? There had to be something that I would like.

So after we ate (I ate every single piece of tofu on my plate) and cleaned up the dishes, Mom set up her laptop in the kitchen. I'm not sure why, but we seem to do everything in the kitchen. It's like if the house had a heart, it would be the kitchen, you know? (Okay, I know that sounds a little weird. Maybe I'm eating too much tofu.)

Anyway, we went on the Park Street Middle School website and clicked on "Activities and Clubs." There was lots of stuff to choose from. We went down the list alphabetically.

"How about the chess club?" Mom asked.

"Boring," I said.

"The drama club?" Mom suggested. "You're

14

very funny, Katie. You're always entertaining your friends."

That was a pretty nice compliment, I thought. But I had one objection. "I can be funny in front of my friends. But on a stage? No way. I would totally freak out."

"Are you sure?" Mom asked. "You don't know until you try."

I tried picturing myself in front of an auditorium full of people, and I got sweaty just thinking about it. "Nope."

"All right," Mom said. "How about the debate team?"

I shook my head. "If I don't want to be funny in front of people, I certainly don't want to debate in front of them. Plus, I'd have to research topics and gather information. You need to put a lot of work into getting your point across."

"Well you certainly did a good job getting your point across that you don't want to debate," Mom said with a smile. "How about the math club?"

"That would be 'no' with a capital *N*," I said.

Mom sighed. "Well, there must be *something* here you'd like to do," she said. "Why don't you take a look?"

As she turned the laptop to face me, the phone

rang. Mom got up from the table and picked up the phone on the wall.

"Hi, Mom," she said, and I knew she was talking to Grandma Carole. "Yes, the girls met today, but we're going to keep your special dessert a secret. No, I won't give you any hints!"

Then Mom took the phone into the living room, and I knew she was trying to talk to Grandma without me hearing. I strained to listen, but Mom was talking in her low phone voice.

Then she came back in the kitchen. "Katie, Grandma wants to talk to you."

I took the phone. "Hi, Grandma."

"Hello, Katie-kins!" Grandma Carole said. She has called me Katie-kins since I can remember, and she is the *only* one who calls me that—so don't get any ideas. "So, your mom tells me you're trying to find an after-school activity you can try."

"Yeah," I said. "But I'm having a hard time."

"What about sports?" Grandma asked.

"Well, I'm not exactly great at sports," I said. "Remember Grandpa's stitches?"

"Accidents happen," Grandma said. "And you're young—like a baby deer finding her legs."

A baby deer? I thought. This conversation was getting a little weird.

"Haven't you ever seen a baby deer on one of those animal shows on TV? At first when they try to walk they are really wobbly. But after just a little while, once they gain confidence, they are frolicking in the woods with all the other deer. You just need practice—and confidence. Maybe you'd feel more comfortable joining a team with your friends. Do your friends play any sports?"

"Mia and Alexis play soccer," I replied. "But I stink at soccer."

"Nonsense!" Grandma Carole said. "Have you ever played before?"

"Well, a couple of times in gym, and—"

"That's all? That's not a true test," she interrupted. "Soccer is a wonderful game. Doesn't it look like fun when you see your friends play?"

"It kind of does," I admitted.

"Life is not worth living if you're always sitting in the stands, Katie," Grandma said. "Go out there and try out for the soccer team. I bet you will surprise yourself."

"Maybe I will," I told her. Grandma Carole was so convincing, I was starting to feel like I could kick a goal from all the way across the field.

"I love you, Katie-kins. Now will you give me a hint about my birthday dessert?"

17

I laughed. "Nice try, Grandma! Not a chance. It's a surprise."

Grandma chuckled. "Okay then. It was worth a shot. Please give me back to your mom."

"Bye, Grandma. Love you, too," I said and then handed the phone to Mom. She was smiling.

I was smiling too. I didn't feel flat anymore. I had a plan. Tomorrow at lunch, I would talk to Mia and Alexis about soccer.

CHAPTER 3

I've Got a Plan

The cafeteria at Park Street Middle School is pretty much like any other cafeteria. Lunch ladies serve food from behind steamy serving tables. It's superloud, and at some point spitballs will be thrown (usually by Eddie Rossi and his friends). And even though the seats aren't marked, everyone sits in the same place every day.

Take the Popular Girls Club (PGC), for example. They have the best table in the cafeteria, the one closest to the lunch line, where you can see everybody who goes by. Sydney Whitman, their blond-haired, blue-eyed leader, always sits in the right corner seat. Her friend Maggie sits next to her, and Bella sits across from Maggie. Callie, my former best friend, sits across from Sydney. The rest of the seats are empty—unless Queen Sydney gives her royal permission for someone to sit there.

Even though Callie's not my best friend anymore, she's still kind of my friend, so I always say hi to her on the way to my table. Callie always says hi back, but Sydney usually rolls her eyes or else she whispers something to Maggie and they laugh. I just ignore them. It makes life easier that way.

Anyway, I think the Cupcake Club table is the best one in the cafeteria even though it's kind of way in the back. But it's a little bit quieter back there, so Mia, Alexis, Emma, and I can talk cupcake business without anybody bothering us. (Well, most of the time. There was that one day when Eddie shot a spitball at us from ten tables away. Gross, but impressive.)

This Wednesday I found Mia at the table. She usually gets there first. Alexis and Emma were in the hot-lunch line, like they always are.

"Hey," I said to Mia, who was opening the lid of her plastic lunch container. I noticed what looked like little pies inside. "Pie for lunch?" I asked.

"They're empanadas," Mia explained. "They're kind of like pies, but they don't have to be sweet. These are chicken and cheese. My dad and I visited my *abuela* last weekend, and she sent me home with a bunch."

Now, I only started taking Spanish this year, but I hang around with Mia enough to know that "*abuela*" means "grandmother."

"Cool. Your grandma bakes too," I said.

"Want a bite?" Mia asked, holding out one of the empanadas.

"Sure," I said. I opened my lunch bag and took out some carrots and some homemade oatmeal cookies. "Only if we can trade."

"Deal," Mia said with a grin.

Alexis and Emma walked up carrying trays of spaghetti and salad.

"I love spaghetti day," Alexis said, sliding into her seat. "It actually tastes like food."

"If the other stuff doesn't taste like food, then what does it taste like?" I asked.

"I'm not sure," Alexis replied. "Alien brains, maybe?"

Emma giggled. "It's not that bad."

Alexis and Emma started to eat their spaghetti. I decided to come right out with my idea. It was all I could think about all morning.

"So, I was talking to my grandma last night," I said.

"About cupcakes?" Alexis asked.

"Not exactly," I answered. "We were talking about why I don't participate in activities, like sports. I know I'm terrible at them, but grandma thought maybe it's because I haven't played a lot. You know, just to have fun."

Emma nodded. "That could be it. I've been playing basketball and Wiffle ball with my mom and dad and my brothers since I was little. Maybe that's why I don't stink at it."

"And in Manhattan, I joined my neighborhood soccer league when I was five," Mia added.

"Yeah, so, I was thinking maybe I could try soccer," I said a little shyly. "I mean, I know I'm no good or anything but—"

"Katie, that would be so cool!" Mia said, her dark eyes shining with excitement. "I would love it if you played with us!"

"Definitely," Alexis agreed. "That would be so much fun if you were on the team!"

"And don't worry about not being good," Mia said quickly. "Alexis and I can help you. Right, Alexis?"

"Of course," Alexis said. "We have a game on Saturday, so maybe that afternoon we could practice with you."

"Perfect!" I said happily.

It made me feel good to see Mia and Alexis so excited about me being on the team. And with their help, maybe I could be a halfway decent player. I actually felt a little bit excited about trying out. Maybe this wouldn't be so bad after all.

"You know, you should come to my house tomorrow after school," Emma said. "You could play some basketball with me and my brothers. Just for fun, like you said. Who knows? If you're good, you could try out for the team next winter."

The idea of playing basketball with anybody—especially teenage boys—would normally make me very nervous. But for some reason I felt like I could actually do it. Maybe my friends' enthusiasm was rubbing off on me.

"Okay," I said.

The little voice inside me was saying, *Basketball? Are you crazy? You couldn't make a basket if you climbed on a ladder!*

It's just for fun, I told the little voice. *I've got to try, just like Grandma said.*

CHAPTER 4

It's Supposed to Be *Touch* Football

There was one thing that Grandma Carole hadn't psyched me up for: gym class. There are lots of reasons why I hate gym class more than any other class, even math:

1. I stink at all sports. (Yes, I'm trying new ones. But right now I stink at most of them.)

2. The teacher, Ms. Chen, has no heart. She's not mean, exactly, but when you mess up, she doesn't say, "Oh, don't worry about it, honey," like my mom would. Instead she says, "Look sharp, Katie!" or "Get it together, Katie!" If Ms. Chen wasn't a gym teacher, I think she would be an ice princess living

in an ice castle, with her glossy black hair pulled back and a white sparkly dress, and everything she touched would turn to ice.

3. Both Sydney *and* Maggie of the Popular Girls Club are in that class, and I only have one friend in gym with me: Emma.

4. Back in September my friend George Martinez started teasing me by calling me "Silly Arms," after that sprinkler thing with the arms that wiggle all over the place, squirting out water. I guess that's what I look like when I play volleyball. Anyway, I didn't mind when George said it, but now other kids call me that too.

So two periods after lunch I was in the gym, wearing my blue shorts and my blue T-shirt that says PARK STREET MIDDLE SCHOOL in yellow writing on the front. Emma and I were sitting on the bleachers, waiting for class to start.

Sydney and Maggie were the last ones out of the locker room. Maggie has frizzy brown hair that's always in her face, but Sydney always manages to look perfect, even in a gym uniform. Her straight, shiny hair is never out of place. I'm not sure how she does it. I think she must have been born that way. I can just picture Sydney as a little baby in the hospital. All the other babies would be screaming and crying, and little Sydney would be quietly smoothing her perfect hair.

Ms. Chen marched out of the gym teacher's office carrying her clipboard, and Sydney walked up to her with a big smile on her face.

"Ms. Chen, what are we doing today?" she asked.

"Flag football," Ms. Chen replied. She nodded over at George Martinez and Ken Watanabe. "George, Ken, get the flags from the supply closet."

"Flag football! Awesome!" Ken shouted. He and George high-fived as they raced to the supply closet.

I groaned as the boys ran off.

"It won't be so bad," Emma said, but she didn't sound convinced.

"Honestly, I will never figure out how to play that stupid game," I said. "Are you supposed to run around and grab other people's flags? Then why is there a ball involved?"

"It's like football, but instead of tackling the player with the ball, you grab their flag," Emma explained.

I shook my head. "You might as well be telling me how to build a rocket right now," I said. "I do not get it. It's too confusing."

"Then just run around and stay away from the ball," Emma suggested.

"Now *that* sounds like a plan," I agreed.

Ms. Chen blew her whistle, and we both jumped up and ran to line up on the black line that goes all around the edges of the gym. Ms. Chen took attendance and then made us warm up with jumping jacks, push-ups, and sit-ups.

I'm pretty good at jumping jacks and sit-ups, but that whole push-up deal is not so easy; maybe because my arms are so skinny. I am usually on my third one while the class is finishing up number ten.

"Look alive there, Katie!" Ms. Chen called out.

Or I will turn you into ice, I thought. *Actually, that wouldn't be so bad. Then I wouldn't have to play flag football.*

Then it was time to choose teams. She made George and Ken captains. George picked me to be on his team, which was nice because he didn't even pick me last. But then he picked Sydney and Maggie, and Ken picked Emma.

"Oh this is great. We're on a team with Katie,"

Sydney said loudly, in a supersarcastic voice.

I looked at Emma across the room.

Help me! I mouthed and then frowned, but all Emma could do was make a sad face back.

We were the red team, so we each had to strap this red belt thing around our waists and then stick a red scarf thing, the flag, in it.

Just stay away from the ball, I kept telling myself. *Everything's going to be all right.*

Boy, was I wrong.

It didn't start out too bad. Our team had the ball first, and George threw it to Wes Kinney, and he ran toward the other team, and Ken chased him and pulled his flag. I didn't have to do anything.

Then the other team had the ball, and Ken threw it to Aziz Aboud, and then Aziz threw it back to Ken, and then Wes grabbed Ken's flag and yelled out, "Revenge!"

Then it was our team's turn again, and before Ms. Chen blew the whistle I saw Sydney whispering to George. Then the play started, and George pretended like he was going to throw the ball to Wes again, only he handed it to Sydney.

I was kind of running around in a circle, minding my own business, when I heard Sydney yell, "Katie! Catch!"

The next thing I knew, I saw a football flying toward my head.

"Ow!" I cried as the ball smacked me on top of the head.

Sydney giggled. "Oops! Sorry, Katie. I guess my aim is off today."

Yeah, right, I thought as I rubbed my sore head.

"Shake it off, Katie!" Ms. Chen yelled.

See what I mean? No sympathy.

Ms. Chen blew her whistle again, and I resumed my plan of running around aimlessly.

Emma ran up to me. "Sydney *so* did that on purpose!" she whispered.

"I know!" I hissed back. "And she doesn't even get in trouble!"

For the next few plays I was Sydney's target. She kept getting the ball, and every time she got it she threw it to me no matter where I was.

"Come on, Silly Arms. Try to catch it!" George called out.

"Yeah, Silly Arms!" Sydney repeated, and she and Maggie burst into giggles.

Wes rolled his eyes. "You guys are so dumb," he said, and I thought he was actually standing up for me. But then he said, "Why would you even throw it to Katie? She can't catch anything. She

29

couldn't catch on fire if she wanted to."

I could feel my cheeks getting red. This game was turning into my worst nightmare. When did it suddenly become "Let's Pick on Katie Day"?

Luckily, the next time Sydney had the ball, Eddie ran up to her and grabbed her flag. Eddie is kind of a jerk, but he's the tallest boy in middle school, and I guess he's pretty handsome. He even grew a mustache last summer, but his mom finally made him shave it off.

Anyway, Sydney got all giggly and pushed into Eddie after he got the flag. The next time Eddie had the ball, Sydney and Maggie chased after him, and then instead of grabbing his flag, they kind of fell into him, and all three of them fell onto the floor.

Ms. Chen blew her whistle. "Break it up, people!"

From then on all Sydney and Maggie wanted was to get the boys' attention, which was fine with me. The next time Sydney got the ball she ran right *at* Eddie and Aziz instead of trying to avoid them. The boys started tackling her, and Sydney started shrieking.

"My hair! You're messing up my hair!"

Ms. Chen blew her whistle. "Eddie! Aziz! On the bench!" she yelled.

Grumbling, the two boys walked to the bleachers. I couldn't believe it. Sydney was the one who started everything, and once again, she didn't get in trouble at all! I know Mom says I shouldn't say "hate" about anyone, but I really do hate Sydney Whitman.

The rest of the game was a mess. Even though the blue team had lost Eddie and Aziz, our team couldn't score because Sydney and Maggie kept bumping into George and Wes and the other boys and giggling.

Finally the game ended.

"Blue team wins by two points!" Ms. Chen announced, and the blue team cheered.

Wes punched me in the arm. "Thanks a lot, Skinny Arms," he said in a mean voice.

"Yeah, thanks for making us lose, Skinny Arms," Maggie added, and everybody on the red team laughed.

Well, everybody but George. "Hey, she's Silly Arms, not Skinny Arms!" he yelled. I gave him a look. Then he came up to me and said, "It wasn't your fault, Katie." But I didn't say anything to him. Everybody else thought I made the team lose, and that was so unfair. It was Sydney's fault! But if I said anything, Sydney's crew would back her up and I'd just end up looking like a sore loser.

I felt like crying, but I didn't because I knew that would only make things worse. So I ran into the locker room without looking back.

I was going to have to get good at sports soon or the rest of my life was going to be miserable.

CHAPTER 5

Outshined by a Kindergarten Kid

The next day after school I walked home with Emma. She seemed really excited. As for me, I wasn't as confident as I had been the other day at lunch. My stomach had been in nervous knots all day. Me, play basketball? What was I thinking?

"This is going to be fun, Katie, I promise," Emma said. "Nothing like gym class."

I wanted to believe her, and I knew that Emma's brothers were basically nice. Jake was in kindergarten, and he's really cute and sweet. Her oldest brother, Sam, is in high school, and he plays sports and works at the movie theater, and he's smart and nice, too.

Then there's Matt, who's one grade above us in

middle school. Alexis had a crush on him a few months ago, and I'm not sure why. I guess he's cute, but he's definitely not as handsome as Sam. And he's a total slob. And sometimes he says mean things to Emma. But most of the time he's pretty nice.

"Okay," I said, taking a deep breath. "Just for fun. I can do that. At least Ms. Chen won't be there telling me to look sharp."

"And Sydney won't be there either," Emma promised. Then she started talking in a silly high voice. "Oh, help! Help! My hair!"

I laughed. Emma is one of those people who never says anything bad about anybody, but Sydney was being so ridiculous lately that even Emma couldn't help it.

"Well, I don't care if my hair gets messed up," I said honestly. "I'd just like to make at least one basket for a change."

"I'm sure you'll do great," Emma said confidently.

When we got to Emma's house, her three brothers were already playing in the driveway. Matt was dribbling a basketball between his legs, and Sam was holding up Jake, so he could make a dunk shot. Jake dropped the ball through the hoop and then clapped his hands.

"I did it!" he cheered.

Sam swung Jake around and put him on the ground. Then he saw me and smiled. "Hey, Katie."

"Hey," I said back, and my heart was beating really fast, and my palms started to get sweaty. I didn't mention this before, because it's kind of embarrassing, but I guess I have kind of a crush on Sam. Mia does too. He's got blond hair, like all of the Taylors, and he always smells nice; not sweaty like Matt. And, I know, he's in high school and I'm in middle school, so I couldn't date him or anything. (Actually, the whole idea of dating kind of terrifies me, anyway.) But still, I can't help how I feel when I'm around him sometimes.

Then Matt ran up to the basket and did one of those shots where you jump up and sink the ball from the side. He was showing off, I think.

"So let's get this game started," he said. "Boys against girls, right?"

"Seriously?" I asked, and I suddenly felt cold and clammy. How were Emma and I supposed to play against two older boys who were practically professionals?

"Don't worry, you can have Jake," Matt said with a grin. He tossed the ball to Emma. "Girls first."

Emma took the ball to a chalk line drawn across the driveway.

"This is the foul line," she explained. "Every time we start, we start from here."

"Got it," I said.

"I've got Katie!" Matt called out, and he ran and stood next to me.

Sam stood facing Emma, blocking her. Jake was running around yelling, "Throw it to me! Throw it to me!"

Sam was a lot bigger than Emma, but Emma was fast. She ducked to the left, and before I knew what was happening, she threw the ball to me!

To my surprise, I caught it. And then . . . I stood there.

"Go to the basket, Katie!" Emma called out.

I turned around and started to dribble the ball. One . . . two . . . and then Matt slapped the ball away from me.

"Oh yeah!" he cried, dribbling up to the basket. Then he sank a shot cleanly through the net.

"Two points!" he cheered, and he and Sam high-fived each other. Then Matt took the ball to the foul line.

"Block him, Katie," Emma instructed me. "Don't let him get past you."

I stood in front of Matt, like I had seen Sam stand before, and kind of spread my arms wide and bent my knees.

"Katie, you look like a gorilla!" Matt teased. "Come on, try and get the banana."

He held up the ball, like he was going to throw it, and I jumped up to block it. Then he darted to the left and bounced the ball toward the basket, sinking another shot.

"And he scores again!" Matt congratulated himself.

"Dude, you're hogging the ball," Sam complained.

"I can't help it if I'm awesome," Matt replied, and Sam punched him playfully in the arm.

Then it was my turn to take the ball to the foul line. Matt was guarding me, and I was really stressed out. Sam was so tall that I couldn't even see Emma, and Jake was running in circles again, yelling, "Me! Me!"

I just stood there, trying to decide what to do. Matt started tapping his foot impatiently.

"Sometime this century, please," he said.

I had no choice. I bounced the ball to Jake, and he caught it! Then he ran up to the basket and chucked the ball underhand with all his might.

The ball rolled around and around on the rim—and then it went in!

"Yay, Jake!" Emma cheered.

Jake ran up and high-fived her. "I'm awesome too!" he bragged.

I was happy for Jake, but even more embarrassed than ever—a kindergarten kid was better than me!

Still, it was kind of fun, even though I was terrible at it. The next time our team got the ball, Emma threw it to me, and Matt accidentally knocked into me while he tried to block me.

"Foul!" Sam yelled. "Katie, you get a free shot from the foul line."

Matt tossed the ball to me, and I stood on the chalk line, facing the basket. Everyone was staring at me, and I could feel my palms getting sweaty again. I wasn't sure if I was holding the ball right or how to shoot. I swung the ball underhand and then let go. The ball soared through the air and . . . crashed into the garbage cans on the other side of the driveway.

"Wrong basket, Katie!" Matt teased, and my face went red.

Sam ran and got the ball. "She gets a do over," he said.

"No fair!" Matt cried. "Why?"

"Because I said so," Sam told him. (Didn't I tell you he was nice?)

Sam stood behind me and reached over my head and put the ball in my hands. I could feel my heart getting all fluttery again. He placed my hands on the right spots on the ball and then he grabbed my arms.

"Pull back, then push up," he said, moving my arms the right way as he talked. "Let go when you're at the top. Don't aim for the basket, aim for the spot on the backboard just above the basket."

What I heard was "Blah, blah, blah, blah, blah" because I couldn't concentrate with Sam so close to me. Then he stepped back.

"Okay, give it a try, Katie," he said. "You can do it!"

I took a deep breath and tried to throw the ball the way Sam showed me. The ball soared through the air . . . and dropped down at least three feet below the basket.

"Painful!" Matt called out. "Better luck next time, Katie."

Sam tried to cheer me up. "Don't worry about it, Katie," he said. "Anybody who can make cupcakes like you can shouldn't worry about whether they can make a basket or not."

"Thanks," I said, but it didn't make me feel much better.

Making cupcakes was not going to help me solve my problem!

CHAPTER 6

What's the Point?

Even though I was terrible at basketball, I didn't give up. I didn't make any baskets at all during the game, but Emma and Jake made some. In the end Sam and Matt beat us by six points.

"Good game, Katie," Matt said, giving me a fist bump. "You looked better the more we played." That's when I figured that his teasing was part of the game, like what my friend George does. He didn't give me a hard time about losing or playing badly, and I was grateful for that.

Then Sam had to leave for work, and Matt had to go to a practice, so Emma and I did our homework in her kitchen while Jake colored next to us.

"So, what did you think?" Emma asked.

"Well, it was kind of fun," I admitted. "But I definitely stink at basketball. There's no way I can try out for the basketball team."

"Oh, you weren't so bad, Katie," Emma said kindly.

I shook my head. "Emma, I tried to make a basket in your garbage cans," I said, laughing. "I'm bad."

Emma started to smile. "Well, maybe you wouldn't be a good fit for the basketball team," she said. "But I hope you'll play with us again sometime."

I thought about Jake being so cute when he made a basket, and Matt goofing around, and Sam showing me how to shoot the ball. . . .

"Sure," I said. "That would be fun."

Then my cell phone rang, and it was my mom calling to tell me she had pulled up outside. I packed up my books in my backpack and said good-bye to Emma and Jake.

I climbed into the car with Mom. Even though she wasn't wearing her dentist jacket, she still smelled a little bit like a dentist's office—a mix of mint and . . . teeth. "Did you have fun?" she asked.

"Yes," I said. "But I stink at basketball. Everything

is still the same. I have no other talent, and I will always be a loser in gym. I don't even know why I'm trying. What's the point?"

"Well, sometimes the point is just to have fun," Mom said. "And I wouldn't give up yet. There are still lots of other things you can try."

"I guess," I said, and I sank down into my seat.

When we got home I helped Mom make dinner—a big salad with chicken and avocadoes and tomatoes and lots of other good stuff in it. Before we sat down to eat, I saw that I had a text from Grandma Carole on my phone.

How is your sports quest going?

I quickly wrote her back.

Terrible. Played basketball today. Couldn't make a basket.

Then I got another text from her.

Keep trying! I am sure you will find your talent.

Maybe. I just hoped I'd find one soon.

Tx Grandma. ♥ you.

She texted me back.

♥ you too Katie-kins!

But even Grandma's texts didn't make me feel better. During dinner I didn't feel like talking much, and so most of the time all you could hear was me and Mom crunching on lettuce. But then Mom had an idea.

"I was thinking of going for a run after dinner," she said. "Do you want to join me?"

I didn't. I was still bruised and sweaty from playing basketball, and besides that I was cranky.

"I just don't get the idea of running," I said. "You run and run and then you end up in the same place where you started. What's the point?"

"The point is that running is really good for your cardiovascular system," Mom said in her I'm-going-to-teach-you-something voice and then she proceeded to tell me how great running is for your health and stuff. It still didn't make me feel like running. "Plus, you just feel great after."

"Not now," I said. "Maybe some other time, okay?"

"Okay," Mom said, and her voice changed. I could tell she knew something was bothering me. "How about when I get back we make some cupcakes? I've got this green-tea recipe I want to try. And if you say 'What's the point?' I'll probably scream."

I had to smile. "There is always a point to making cupcakes," I said, and I realized I meant it. Even if baking cupcakes didn't help me be good at sports, at least it was something I was good at. And that was something to be proud of, right?

Even Sam thought so.

CHAPTER 7

I Hate to Admit It, but Sydney Is Right

$\mathcal{M}$om and I made a batch of green-tea cupcakes with cinnamon and other stuff in the icing. The green tea tasted weird and good at the same time, and the sweet cinnamon icing tasted really good with it. I brought four cupcakes into school the next day—Cupcake Friday.

I decided to have some fun with the cupcakes. When we were done eating lunch, I handed one to each of my friends.

"Okay, welcome to everyone's favorite game show, *Guess That Cupcake!*" I said, using the banana from my lunch as a microphone. "Take a bite and see if you can guess what flavor it is!"

Alexis answered first. "No idea, but it's green, so . . . cucumber?"

I shook my head. "Nope! Emma?"

"Um, maple?" Emma answered.

"Not maple," I told her. I turned to Mia. She was taking a second bite, and she had a thoughtful look on her face.

"Hmm," she said, thinking out loud. "I think this is . . . green tea."

"You are correct!" I cried. "How did you know?"

"My dad and I get green tea when we go out for sushi," Mia replied. "So what do I win?"

Whoops! I hadn't thought of that. I handed her the banana. "You win this delicious banana!"

"A banana? I've always dreamed of owning a banana," Mia joked, and I laughed with her.

"So is this a flavor your grandma likes?" Alexis asked, opening her notebook.

"No, that's just something my mom wanted to try," I replied. I reached into my lunch bag and pulled out a piece of paper. "I made a list of Grandma Carole's favorite flavors last night."

Alexis took the list from me. She looked impressed. "Thanks."

"Maybe Alexis is rubbing off on you," Emma suggested.

Alexis turned over the list. "Katie, this is written

47

on the back of your math quiz," she said.

I shrugged. "I'm recycling. Anyway, check it out. There're some good flavors in there."

"Blueberry, chocolate, raspberry, lime, and . . . chubby?" Alexis asked.

"That's *cherry*," I said. "Although chubby cupcakes would be awfully cute, wouldn't they?"

Alexis sighed. "I think there are some good flavor combinations here," she said. "We need a baking session. How about Sunday?"

"That's perfect," Mia said. "Because tomorrow we'll be teaching Katie how to play soccer before our game."

I had almost forgotten about that. "Oh yeah, sure."

Then I heard a loud voice behind me.

"Watch out for Silly Arms, Mia." It was Sydney, of course. "She'll spill her lunch all over that designer sweater you're wearing."

I turned and saw that Sydney was standing with the whole PGC—Maggie and Bella, who were giggling, and Callie, who looked like she wanted to sink into the floor.

"I'm not worried, Sydney," Mia said. She's one of the only girls in school who can stand up to Sydney. They were kind of friends, once, but I don't think that worked out too well.

Sydney rolled her eyes. "Have you seen this girl in gym? Loser! She's a safety hazard. The school should make her wear a helmet just to walk down the hall."

"There are no losers at this table," Mia said, and she looked angry. "I think you need to apologize to my friend."

Mia is so brave! I love her so much. I wanted to hug her. Then Callie spoke up, and I thought she was going to defend me too. After all, we were best friends for, like, twelve years. But instead she just tried to distract Sydney.

"Hey, Syd, Eddie Rossi told me he wanted to talk to you before," she said.

Sydney took the bait. "Really?"

"Yeah, I think we should go see him now," Callie told her.

"Bye, Mia," Sydney said, as if she had just been talking about tuna fish instead of insulting me.

Sydney marched off across the lunchroom and Callie and the rest of the PGC followed her. Callie kind of glanced over her shoulder at me with a worried look, but I just turned away. I guess by distracting Sydney she was trying to help me out, but frankly it just didn't seem like enough.

"Oh, Katie, Sydney is just awful!" Emma cried.

"Don't worry," Alexis said. "One day, when we're all cupcake millionaires, we'll buy a big billboard that says 'Sydney Is a Loser.'"

I turned to Mia. "You are awesome for standing up for me. Thanks."

"It's okay, Katie," Mia said. "You're the one who's awesome. Don't listen to her. She doesn't know what she's talking about."

"Actually, she does," I pointed out. "She's right. I'm a total spaz. I probably should wear a helmet."

"You're letting her psych you out," Mia said. "You'll see. Tomorrow, when we play soccer, you'll see you're not a spaz."

"I really hope so," I said. "You know, I started out just wanting to be good at something besides cupcakes. But now I feel like I've got something to prove. I'll never get through middle school and high school if I can't get through gym. I'm tired of being teased, you know?"

My friends nodded sympathetically. Alexis was punching in numbers on a calculator with a serious expression on her face. Then she looked up and smiled.

"The way I see it, there's about an eighty percent

chance that you'll be good in at least one sport," she said. "Maybe it will be soccer. I haven't worked out the numbers for that yet."

"Those odds sound pretty good to me," I said. "Just keep your fingers crossed. Or else the next six years of my life will be totally miserable!"

CHAPTER 8

I Discover My Secret Skill

You can do it, Katie-kins!

I tried to imagine Grandma Carole's voice cheering me on as Mom drove me to Mia's house for my soccer lesson.

"I'll pick you up at four, okay?" Mom asked as we pulled up in front of the big white house.

"Okay," I replied. "Hopefully I won't have some freak soccer ball accident and end up in the hospital or anything."

"Don't worry. I'm sure you'll do fine," Mom said. "Just remember to have fun! And don't forget to wear your mouth guard!" With a mom as a dentist, I practically have to wear a mouth guard to walk down the hall.

Remember to have fun. Who says that? Moms,

that's who. Why on Earth would someone have to remind you to have fun? Shouldn't fun just . . . happen?

I heard noises coming from Mia's backyard, and when I walked back there, I saw Mia and Alexis. Alexis was setting up orange cones all over the biggest part of the yard. In the side yard next to the garage, Mia's stepbrother, Dan, and some other guy were playing catch with a softball.

Alexis marched up to me. Like Mia, she was wearing her red soccer shorts and her practice T-shirt. But Alexis had a whistle around her neck and a clipboard in her hand.

"Okay, so we're going to start with some drills," she said crisply.

I had to laugh. Alexis sure loves being in charge—no matter what is going on.

"Um, hi, Alexis, nice to see you, too," I said.

She gave a slightly embarrassed smile. "Sorry, Katie, don't mean to get carried away. It's just kind of fun getting to be a coach instead of listening to a coach, you know?"

"Anyway, drills are a good idea," Mia chimed in. "That's how we start all our practices."

I looked at the cones, which were arranged in a kind of zigzag pattern all the way across the lawn. "So what do I have to do exactly?"

"You just kick the ball around the cones," Mia said. "Like this."

She started dribbling the ball, kicking it a short way and then running after it and kicking it some more. She wove around all of the cones perfectly. The way she did it, it looked kind of easy.

"Okay," I said. "I'll try it."

Mia kicked the ball to me, and I gave it a kick. It went skidding across the grass, nowhere near the cones.

"Just small kicks," Alexis said. "And kick with the inside of your foot, not the toe."

She ran after the ball and dribbled it back. I saw what she was talking about.

"Cool," I said. "Here we go."

I kicked the ball like Alexis had shown me, and it didn't go sailing away this time. I kicked it toward the first cone—and knocked the cone right over.

"That's okay, Katie!" Mia called out. "Keep going."

I made my way to the second cone, but this time I tripped when I was trying to kick the ball. I stumbled into the cone and knocked that one down too.

I was starting to get discouraged, but I could hear Grandma Carole inside my head.

Keep trying!

So I gave it my best. I promise you. But I barely made it through the course. By the time I got to the last cone, I had knocked over almost every one.

"If this was a game where you got points for knocking down cones, I'd be an all-star," I joked.

"Don't worry, Katie," Mia said, trying to keep me from being too discouraged. "Nobody gets it the very first time they try."

"It just takes practice," Alexis said. "I would recommend going through the course four or five more times."

Mia must have seen the look of horror on my face. "Or how about a kicking lesson?" she said. "We can practice passing. We'll kick the ball back and forth to each other as we make our way down the field."

"Okay," I said. "As long as there are no cones involved, I should be fine."

Once again Mia and Alexis demonstrated for me. They each got on opposite sides of the yard, and Mia kicked the ball hard. It skidded across the grass in an almost perfect straight line to Alexis.

"Okay, now I'll kick it to you, Katie," Alexis said. "And you can kick it to Mia."

"I'm ready!" I called out, trying to sound confident.

Alexis kicked the ball, and I ran to meet it. Then I kicked it as hard as I could in Mia's direction.

Only the ball did not go in Mia's direction. Instead it sailed backward, over my head, and bounced into the side yard where Dan and his friend were playing catch. Dan's friend ran to get the ball.

"Sorry!" I called out.

"Hey!" Dan called out in a teasing voice. "Now we're going to throw our ball at you!"

He lobbed the softball right at me, and I reached up and something amazing happened: I caught it!

Then something even more amazing happened. Without even thinking I threw the ball back to Dan. The ball did not fly backward over my head. It did not knock over any cones or garbage cans. Instead the ball soared in a beautiful arc and landed right in Dan's glove!

"Hey, you've got a pretty good arm," Dan said, and he sounded impressed. "Are you on the softball team?"

"Um, no," I answered shyly. "I've actually never played softball before."

"Really?" Mia asked, running up next to me.

I thought about it. "Well, sometimes we play Wiffle ball in gym. But I always stand way, way back in the outfield. And usually the guys think I can't catch the ball, so if it comes to me, they jump in front of me and catch it."

Alexis looked confused. "I don't get it, Katie. You can't catch or throw a football like that. So why did you catch that softball?"

I shrugged. "I don't know. Footballs are kind of . . . wobbly," I guessed. "They confuse me."

"Maybe it's because a softball is more cupcake-size," Mia teased. "It's got to be cupcake related somehow."

"It doesn't really matter *why* you can do it," Alexis said, and she sounded excited. "You *can* do it! And it's spring, which means that softball tryouts start soon. Katie, I think you've found your talent."

It seemed too good to be true that I could actually be good at a sport. Maybe my catching and throwing the ball perfectly was a fluke, a one-time thing.

"Let's make sure," I said. I called out to the guys. "Dan! Over here!"

Dan threw the ball to me again, and once again, I caught it. I grinned.

I had finally found my secret skill.

CHAPTER 9

So Running Isn't So Bad After All

$\mathcal{T}$he first thing I did when I got home was call Grandma Carole.

"Hi, Grandma. It's me, Katie," I said.

"Katie-kins! What a nice surprise. Is everything all right?" Grandma asked.

"More than all right, Grandma," I said. "I found a sport I'm actually good at! I'm going to try out for the softball team!"

"Good for you, Katie-kins! I love softball. I bet you'll be hitting home runs out of the park in no time!" Grandma said. I could hear the excitement in her voice.

"Oh . . . ," I said.

"What's the matter?" Grandma asked.

"Well, you just reminded me of something.

I might be good at catching and throwing the ball, but I didn't really think about the hitting part."

"You'll be fine," Grandma said. "You just need a little practice, that's all."

"You sound so sure," I said.

"That's because I *am* sure. I can't wait to see you and hear all about it in person."

"Thanks, Grandma!" I said. "I can't wait to see you too! Love you!"

"Love you, too," Grandma said. "See you soon. Bye!"

I hung up the phone and tried to think positive, the way Grandma always did. But what I was actually thinking about was whiffle ball. Whenever we played whiffle ball at school, I always struck out. I started to feel nervous, but I knew I couldn't back out now.

"I'm very excited for you, Katie," Mom said as we ate our usual Saturday night pizza with mushrooms-and-sausage topping.

"But what if I don't make the team?" I worried. "Everyone's expecting me to become this great softball player. You should have seen the way everybody reacted when I caught and threw the ball."

"I don't think that's the case," Mom said. "Everyone's happy that you found something you're good at and that you like to do. If you don't make the team, at least you know you did your best."

I know Mom was trying to make me feel better, but a slow feeling of panic kept creeping up on me. "I need to start training, like, now," I said. "Can we play catch after dinner?"

"We could, but we don't have any balls or mitts," Mom pointed out. "I'm sure your friends will help you out. In the meantime why don't you go on a run with me tomorrow morning? That will definitely help you get in shape for the tryout."

Just the idea of running seemed superboring, but I knew Mom was right. And I was anxious to start doing something to help me train.

"All right," I said. "But maybe just a few blocks, okay?"

Mom smiled. "We'll see."

The next morning I was sound asleep when Mom came into my room and pulled open the curtains. The bright spring sunshine hit my face, and I groaned and rolled over.

"Rise and shine, Katie!" Mom sang. "It's time for our run!"

"Seriously?" I asked. "The birds aren't even awake yet."

"This is the best time for a run, trust me," Mom said. "Put on some shorts and your good sneakers, and I'll meet you in the kitchen."

I was still pretty sleepy when Mom and I left the house. Mom started jogging, not too fast, and I could keep up with her easily.

I'm not usually an early riser, but I must say it was nice to be up when most of the neighborhood was still asleep. And the air smelled so nice and clean! The sun had just come up, and everyone's lawn was sparkling with morning dew.

I was wrong about the birds. They were all awake, and I had to admit that all the singing and chirping they were doing was kind of pretty. Otherwise, the streets were pretty quiet, because most people were still sleeping.

We jogged down our street and then made a right and headed for the town park. I used to go on the swings and slide there when I was little, but I never noticed the path that went all around the park, weaving around the trees. I saw two squirrels chasing each other around a tree, and a big yellow butterfly, and then there was this bubbling creek we ran past that I didn't even know was in the park.

When we left the park I was sweating a lot and panting a little.

"Wanna go back?" Mom asked me.

To my surprise I didn't. I was actually liking this.

"No," I said. "Let's keep going."

In the end I had to walk the last few blocks home, but Mom said that was good, because we needed to cool down, anyway. My leg muscles hurt, but at the same time I felt good, like I was ready for anything.

"Thanks for coming out with me," Mom said. "Maybe we can do this again sometime."

"Definitely," I agreed.

Then I took a shower, which felt awesome, and then Mom and I went to Sally's Pancake House where I got a short stack of chocolate-chip pancakes, which tasted superdelicious. In the afternoon Mom drove me to Emma's for our cupcake baking session.

Before we make a cupcake for a client, we always test out the recipe first. We use the money from our profits to buy supplies and stuff, and whatever's left over we split among the four of us. We also take turns doing the baking at one another's houses.

At the end of our Friday meeting we had

decided to test a blueberry cupcake and a choco-late raspberry cupcake. When I entered Emma's kitchen, Alexis was already there, setting out the bowls and measuring spoons on Emma's big kitchen table. Emma was taking ingredients out of the blue plastic tub that we use to store our basic stuff.

I didn't see Sam anywhere, but I figured he was working. (And I would never ask where he was—that would just be too embarrassing.) I did see Jake. He was up on a chair, leaning over the table, so he could grab blueberries from the bowl.

Emma shook her head at him. "No, Jake! Those are for the cupcakes."

"There's plenty here for one batch," I said. I took a few blueberries from the bowl and gave them to Jake. "You can have these, and then you can have a cupcake when they're done."

"Thanks!" Jake said happily, and then he left the kitchen as Mia came in.

"My stepdad got all the really ugly wallpaper off of the walls!" she announced happily. "Now I just have to decide what color to paint my room."

"How about rainbow?" I suggested. "With stripes all across the wall."

"Or pink," Emma said. That's Emma's favorite color.

"I like white or cream walls," Alexis said. "It looks neat, and you can always decorate with posters or pictures."

Mia sat down on one of the stools around the counter. "It's just so hard to decide. I'm thinking maybe pale pink with an accent wall, or some kind of purple." Then she noticed all the cupcake supplies on the counter. "But enough about my room. We have cupcakes to design, right?"

"Right," Alexis agreed, getting down to business. "We're going to do some vanilla cupcakes with blueberry jam centers and vanilla frosting with fresh blueberries on top. Then there's a chocolate raspberry cupcake with chocolate frosting and fresh raspberries."

"They both sound *sooo* good," Mia said. "You know, I've been so busy worrying about my room that I forgot to come up with decorating ideas."

"I had one," Alexis said. "Since Katie's grandma likes sports so much, we could do the blueberry cupcakes, but instead of putting blueberries on top, we could decorate them to look like different kinds of balls. Like a soccer ball cupcake and a baseball cupcake, and we could dye the icing green to make a tennis ball cupcake too."

"That's pretty cool," Emma said.

"Definitely," I agreed. "I'm just wondering if it feels adult enough. Soccer-ball cupcakes and baseball cupcakes sound like something Jake would like, you know?"

"I see what you mean," Mia chimed in. "It's great for a kid's party, but maybe not a seventy-fifth birthday celebration."

Alexis nodded. "Yeah, that makes sense," she said. "But I will definitely put this idea in my kids' party file."

"I thought of something," said Emma shyly. "Your grandma was born right at the start of spring, so maybe we can do a spring theme. We could put birds and flowers on the cupcakes."

"That would be so pretty!" Mia said. "I can just picture it!"

"That does sound really nice," I agreed. "And I think that would go nicely with the blueberry cupcakes."

"And maybe the icing could be blue, like a robin's egg," Emma added.

"That is so perfect because Grandma Carole

always looks for the first robin of spring," I said. "She says it's good luck."

"I like it," Alexis said. "Okay, so let's scrap the chocolate raspberry for now. Mia, do you think you can come up with a flowers and birds design?"

"Sure," Mia said, nodding her head. "Maybe I can play with the icing today. We have blue food coloring, right?"

Alexis grabbed the bottle from the table. "Check," she said, holding it up. "Okay, so we have a plan."

For the next couple of hours we worked on our sample cupcakes. We made some basic vanilla batter, and when the cupcakes cooled, I got to use one of my favorite cupcake tools. It's a special tip you can put on the end of a pastry bag. You fill the bag with jam and then stick the tip into the cupcake. One squeeze, and your cupcake has a delicious jam-filled center.

We tested the cupcakes without frosting first.

"Yummy," Alexis said. "But tell me again why we're not using real blueberries in the batter?"

"We could, but it's tricky," I told her. "Since the blueberries are heavier than the batter, usually they fall to the bottom. You can coat them in flour first, but that doesn't always work."

"The blueberry jam is delicious," Mia remarked. "These kind of remind me of that peanut-butter-and-jelly cupcake your mom made for you on the first day of school."

Emma smiled. "Yeah, that cupcake sort of started everything, didn't it?"

"I guess it did," I said. I looked down at Jake, who had blue jam all over his face. "What do you think, Jake?"

"Awesome!" Jake replied.

"Okay, I've got two icings going," Mia said. "One is vanilla with mashed-up blueberries mixed in. The other just has blue food coloring."

The food coloring one looked pretty, just like a robin's egg. The blueberry one looked a little weird. It was more purple than blue, and there were some big blueberry chunks in it. But it tasted really, really good.

"I can't decide," I said. "One is the perfect color, but the other one tastes superamazing."

"I can't decide either," Emma agreed.

"There must be a way to combine them," Alexis suggested. "Katie, maybe your mom can help us. She is, like, the queen of cupcakes."

"And I am the cupcake captain, don't forget," I joked. "But, yeah, I'll definitely ask her."

Then I remembered something. "I need a favor from you guys," I said. "After we clean up."

"What is it?" Emma asked.

I grinned. "Wanna play catch?"

CHAPTER 10

Callie's Mad at *Me*? Seriously?

"Wow, it's true, Katie," Mia said as I tossed a softball to her from across Emma's backyard. "You really can play softball."

"Don't sound so surprised," I joked.

"You know what I mean," Mia shot back.

"I know," I said. "But it's not such a big deal. I can throw and catch. I'm not so sure if I can hit the ball."

"I'm sure Matt will help you with that," Emma said. "As long as you bribe him with cupcakes."

I was secretly hoping she would suggest Sam as a softball coach, but Matt would have to do.

"Sure," I said. "We can give him some blueberry cupcakes from today as a down payment."

Alexis looked at her watch. "Hey, I've got to get

home. We're having dinner early, and I want to get a good night's sleep tonight. We have a big game tomorrow."

"Where is it?" I asked. "Maybe I'll come."

Because I'm not good at sports, I have never much liked watching games on TV or in person. But my friends had been helping me so much, I felt like I had to support them.

"Cool!" Mia said. "It's at the middle-school field at six."

Mom said I could go to the game as long as I finished my homework. On Monday my mom had Joanne, who works with her at her office, pick me up after school. Joanne does that a lot because Mom still doesn't like me being home alone all that much. She took me to Mom's office, and I did my homework with the sound of dentists' drills in the background. I shuddered. Honestly I hate going to the dentist even though the dentist is my mom. But nobody was screaming or crying or anything, so I guess Mom was doing a good job. When Mom finished with her patients she dropped me off at the field.

It's a little weird going to a soccer game when you're not playing, because almost everyone watching is a parent or else a little kid who's been dragged to the game. In the stands I saw Mia's stepdad, Eddie, sitting with Alexis's mom, and I waved hi.

Then I heard a voice calling to me.

"Katie! Over here!"

It was Callie's mom. Mrs. Wilson and my mom have been friends since before Callie and I were born. She's almost like a second mom to me, which is why it's extra weird that Callie and I aren't best friends anymore. I kind of miss seeing her all the time.

So I walked over. "Hi, Mrs. Wilson," I said.

"Hi, Katie." She gave me a hug. "Are you here to see Callie play?"

Uh-oh. Tough question. "Well, sure, and I have two other friends on the team too," I said, only lying just a little bit. "Mia and Alexis."

"Oh yes, they're good players," Mrs. Wilson said. "Come here, have a seat. I haven't seen you in so long."

So I ended up sitting next to Mrs. Wilson for the whole game. That was good, I guess, because she explained a lot of the soccer stuff to me. Like how in the spring league the girls played other teams from Maple Grove. And how many points you got

72

for scoring a goal and who could be on what side of the field when and stuff like that. It all sounded pretty complicated. Maybe it was a good thing I wasn't good at soccer!

Still, the game was pretty exciting. The ball kept going up and down the field. I noticed that Alexis was a really good kicker. She could kick the ball really far and fast. And I cheered when Mia made a goal.

I was kind of surprised to realize that Callie was the star of the team. She was superfast, and whenever someone passed her the ball, she was right on it. And she scored four goals! It was amazing. I cheered for her, too, and I think she heard me because she looked up. But mostly she concentrated on the game.

Even though the Rockets rocked, the other team, the Comets, beat them 8–7. At the end of the game the two teams lined up and then slapped hands as they walked past one another. I thought the Rockets would look sad, but when I ran up to Mia and Alexis after the game they looked pretty psyched.

"Alexis, that pass you made was amazing," Mia was saying.

"Thanks!" Alexis said, high-fiving her. "I think

this was our best passing game ever."

"You did great, guys," I told them. "Soccer looks pretty fun."

"It is," Mia said. "I'm glad you came."

Then Callie walked over, and she looked kind of mad. At first I thought it was because of losing the game. But it turned out she was mad at *me*.

"Katie, what are you doing here?" Callie asked. "You hate sports."

"Maybe I used to," I said, getting defensive. "But not now."

Callie shook her head. "I used to ask you to come to my games all the time. . . ." She looked at Mia and Alexis.

I couldn't believe what she was saying. *Yeah, and I was your best friend until you sold me out to be part of the Popular Girls Club,* I wanted to scream. Not to mention how just the other day she stood by while Sydney made fun of me, and she didn't say a thing! She had no right to be mad at me for this, not even a little.

"We all cheer for one another," Mia said, and she smiled at me. "And it's true, she's really good at softball."

"Yeah, she's even trying out for the team," Alexis said proudly.

74

Callie looked surprised and then she didn't look so mad anymore.

"Really? Wow, that's pretty cool, Katie," she said. "Good luck."

"Thanks," I said. "And good game. I can't believe how many goals you made."

Callie actually smiled. "Thanks," she said. She looked around, and I wondered if she was looking for her new friends, but there were just a lot of parents waiting around. "See you!" She waved, and then she ran off to see her mom.

"That is one complicated situation," Mia said, looking after Callie.

I shrugged. "I guess," I said. "But right now I'm a lot more worried about that softball tryout!"

Especially now that Callie knows I'm trying out, I thought. *If I don't make the team, I am going to look like a loser!*

CHAPTER 11

I'm Keeping My Eye on the Ball, I Swear!

"All right, Katie," Matt said. "Like I showed you. Bend your knees and hold the bat just below your shoulders."

"She's holding it too high!" Alexis said directly behind me.

It was Friday afternoon, the day before tryouts, and Emma had finally arranged to have Matt give me a batting lesson. During the week I ran with Mom a few times after work, and Mom got us a ball and gloves so we could practice catching. But so far, no batting.

And in case you're wondering what Alexis was doing there, she offered to come along and help.

"You can't have batting practice without a

catcher," she said, and I know she's right. But sometimes I wonder if she's really over her crush on Matt.

To be fair, though, Alexis seemed a lot more interested in telling me how to bat than she did in flirting with Matt.

"I am *not* holding it too high," I protested.

"She's good," Matt called back. "Okay, Katie, now keep your eye on the ball!"

"Sure," I said, but actually, I have a problem with that advice. Because when the ball comes at me, it's spinning really fast and it's all blurry and it just makes me nervous.

Then Matt pitched the ball to me underhand, like they do in softball, and I kept my eye on it, I swear—both eyes, even. And when it got close to me I freaked out a little and swung the bat way too soon.

Whump! I heard the ball land in Alexis's catcher's mitt.

"Steeeeee-rike!" Alexis cried, like some professional umpire.

"Too soon, Katie!" Matt called out.

"Yeah, too soon, Katie!" Alexis repeated.

"I know!" I said, a little frustrated. "It's hard to know when to swing."

Matt walked up to me and Alexis. "Okay, how about this?" he asked. "When you think you want to swing, don't. Count to two and then swing, okay?"

"Okay," I said, nodding. Then I got back into batting stance.

"Oh, you are holding it a little too high," Matt said. "Here, move your elbows, like this."

Matt got behind me and positioned my arms— sort of like when Sam was showing me how to shoot a basket. But I didn't have any heart palpitations or sweaty palms this time.

Is that all it means to have a crush on someone? I wondered. Sweaty palms? Would Alexis get sweaty palms if she were standing here now?

"Earth to Katie," Matt said. "Are you listening?"

"Oh, sure," I said. I placed my arms in the right position. "Like this, right?"

"Okay, let's give it another try," Matt said. "This time, count to two before you swing."

"Got it," I said.

Matt pitched the ball to me again. I kept my eye on the ball, and when it got close, I freaked out again.

"Strike!" Alexis cried.

"Why is it that it's good to get a strike in bowling

but bad to get one in baseball?" I wondered out loud, trying to distract Alexis and Matt from the fact that I was terrible.

"Well, this isn't bowling," Alexis said. "I know you can do this. Just keep your eye on the ball."

"I am. I swear," I protested. "That's not the problem."

"What happened to counting to two?" Matt called out.

"I get too nervous," I answered. "When the ball starts to get close, I feel like it's going to hit me in the face or something. So I swing."

"I am not going to throw the ball at your face. I promise," Matt said, rolling his eyes. "Geez!" Then he muttered "Girls!" in an exasperated voice.

"Hey, I heard that!" Alexis called out. "Katie's just nervous, that's all. This has nothing to do with her being a girl."

"That's right!" I agreed. Now I had something to prove. "Let's do this."

Matt pitched. I kept my eye on the ball. When the ball got close, I started counting.

One Mississippi, two Mississippi . . .

Thump! The ball landed in Alexis's glove before I could even swing.

79

"Ball one!" Alexis yelled.

"What does that even mean?" I said.

Matt shook his head. "Katie, I said count to two, not count to two million."

"I *did* count to two," I told him. "I counted by Mississippis."

"Well, no wonder," Alexis said. "That's way too long, Katie."

Matt gave an exasperated sigh. "Forget about counting. Just hit the ball when it gets close to the bat, okay?"

"Got it," I said. I got back into batting stance, more determined than ever.

Do not freak out. Do not freak out, I told myself. *Matt will not hit you in the face.*

Matt pitched. The ball soared through the air. I swung.

Crack! I hit the ball! It went careening to the left, and Alexis ran after it.

I started jumping up and down. "I hit it! I hit it! I hit it!"

"That was a foul ball," Alexis said, running back to me.

"Good job, Katie!" Matt said, and I felt like I was going to burst with pride. "Now next time straighten it out, okay?"

"Okay," I said, even though I had no idea what that meant.

So Matt pitched the ball a bunch more times. And after a while, I sort of got used to the ball coming straight at me. I lost my fear and just concentrated on trying to follow it with my eyes and hit it when it got close. I struck out a few times, and I had a lot more foul balls. But I "straightened out" after Matt showed me how, so I also hit a few good balls. One of them popped up in the air, and Matt caught it. But another one rolled on the grass, and Matt had to chase after it.

Finally Matt called it quits. "You're doing good, Katie. You'll be fine at the tryouts, I think," he said. "Just keep throwing and catching like you do."

"Thanks," I said.

He held out his hand. "And now I believe there was a payment involved?"

I walked over to the Taylors' deck and picked up the box I had brought with me.

"One dozen chocolate peanut-butter cupcakes," I said.

Matt smiled and took the box. "You are the best, Katie."

"Thanks," I said. "You are, too. And so is Alexis. She's a great catcher."

(Did you see what I was doing there? Just trying to help out a friend—just in case Alexis was still getting sweaty palms.)

"Yeah, thanks," Matt said. He turned and smiled at Alexis. "You can play on my team anytime."

Alexis blushed, and I felt like I had done a good deed.

In fact, I was feeling pretty good when Mom took me home. And Mom had a weird smile on her face, like she was keeping a secret.

"A package came for you today," she said as she unlocked the door.

"Really?" I asked. "What is it?"

"I'll let you open it yourself," Mom said, and she handed me a box that looked like a shoebox. I looked at the name on the return address: Carole Hamilton.

"It's from Grandma Carole," I said. Then I ran to the kitchen to get scissors, so I could cut through the tape.

The box was filled with crumpled-up newspaper. I felt around and pulled out a softball. There was a note on a small piece of blue paper.

Dear Katie-kins,

I am so excited that you are going to be on the softball team! I know you're going to do great.

This is a softball I saved from my high school championship team. It's very special to me, and I know it will bring you luck.

Love,

Grandma Carole

"Wow," was all I could say.

Mom read the note over my shoulder. "That's very special," she said.

I tossed the softball from hand to hand, thinking. Grandma Carole was counting on me to get on the team. I didn't want to disappoint her—or Mom or the Cupcake Club or Callie or even Matt.

83

I *had* to get on that team. Failure was not an option. But first I had to get rid of this nervous energy.

"Hey, Mom," I said. "Want to go for a run?"

CHAPTER 12

I Don't Totally Stink

Tryouts were Saturday morning at ten at the middle-school field. I was so nervous that I woke up at five a.m. Mom was still asleep, so I went down to the living room and stared at the ceiling until she woke up.

"Katie, you're up early," she said, yawning. "I'm going to make some coffee. What would you like for breakfast?"

My stomach felt like it was tied in a knot. "I don't think I can eat," I replied.

"You have to eat something," Mom said. "You need energy for your tryouts."

I groaned. I know she was right. "Then I guess, cereal, please."

I munched on a bowl of Grainy Flakes and

changed into shorts and a T-shirt for the tryouts. When we got to the field, there were a lot of girls and parents there. Most of them were lined up in front of a folding table set up over by the stands with a sign that read PARK STREET SOFTBALL TRYOUTS.

"I guess we should get in line," Mom said, so we did.

When we got to the front of the line, we saw a woman about Mom's age wearing a white polo shirt with a whistle around her neck. She had blond hair pulled back in a ponytail.

"Hi, I'm Coach Kendall," she said. Then she nodded to a young guy with brown hair bringing some equipment out of the locker room. "That's Coach Adani. We'll be running the tryouts today. I just need your name, age, and grade on the form, okay?"

I nodded, too nervous to say anything, and filled out the form. I forgot that anyone at Park Street could try out. There would be girls older than me too. Ones that had been playing longer. I gulped.

"I'll head for the stands," Mom said. "Good luck, Katie."

I'm sure she wanted to give me a hug, but

thank goodness she just waved and started walking away.

I headed for the baseball diamond on the field, where most of the girls seemed to be going. I recognized a few girls from my grade. There were Sophie and Lucy, who are nice but they're best, best friends and pretty much only hang out with each other. I saw Beth Suzuki, a girl from my Spanish class who trades notes with me sometimes. And then I saw Maggie Rodriguez from the Popular Girls Club.

I groaned. Just like gym class! She was going to give me a hard time, I just knew it.

But so far, Maggie didn't seem to notice me. In fact, I thought she looked as nervous as I did. She was kind of hanging off to the side and not talking to anybody, which was fine by me.

Before I could think too much about it, Coach Kendall and Coach Adani walked onto the diamond, and Coach Kendall blew her whistle.

"All right girls, line up!" she called, and we quickly got into a line.

"Coach Adani and I are going to put you through some drills today to see what you can do," she said. "First up, I want to see you run around those bases. Don't stop until I tell you. Let's go!"

I relaxed a little bit. Running—I could do that. Sophie was at the head of the line, and she started leading us around the diamond. For a while we all stayed in line. But then it was obvious that some of us were faster and some of us were slower. Without even realizing it, I was at the front of the line, right next to Beth.

We must have gone around about four times when Coach Kendall finally blew the whistle for us to stop. I stepped on home plate, and my heart was pounding. The run had me feeling good, and it also felt good to know that I was one of the fastest on the team. I couldn't help noticing that Maggie was the last one to finish, and she looked really winded.

"All right," Coach Kendall said. "Now we're going to try some fielding." She pointed to me, Beth, and another girl who I didn't know. "I want you to each take a base."

I started to feel nervous all over again. Beth ran to first base, so I took second, and the other girl took third. Coach Adani stood at home plate, and Coach Kendall stood behind him with a catcher's mitt.

"Here's how it's going to work," he said. "I'm going to hit out a ball. If it comes to you, catch it and throw it home."

This is it, I thought. *This is where I prove myself. Can I do it?*

Then I heard cheers from the stands.

"Go, Katie!"

I looked up and saw Alexis and Emma. I knew Mia was at her dad's in Manhattan or else she would be there too. I had my very own cheering section, and I couldn't let them down.

I put my hands on my knees and focused on Coach Adani. He hit a ground ball to Beth. She scooped it up and threw it back to Coach Kendall. The throw was a little wide, and Coach had to chase after it.

Then Coach Adani hit a pop-up to second base. Easy. I caught it and threw it to Coach Kendall— and it landed right in her glove.

I had aced it! I didn't feel so nervous after that. Coach Adani hit two more balls to each of us, and I caught each one that went to me. Then we left the field and the other girls got a turn.

I sat on the grass and watched the competition. Some of the girls, like Lucy, were really good. But a few girls couldn't catch very well. And Maggie . . .

well, Maggie was pretty terrible. But you could see that she was trying really hard.

Maggie missed the first two balls, and when she threw them back, they didn't go anywhere near home plate. And then when Coach Adani hit the third ball to Maggie, it went way to the left. Maggie actually jumped and then dove to catch it! It was pretty cool, and everybody cheered even though the ball ended up bouncing out of her mitt.

As I watched the rest of the fielding tryouts, I felt more and more nervous each minute. I knew what had to be next: batting.

And that's exactly what happened next. Coach Kendall put me and two other girls on the bases while the first group of girls came up to bat. Lucy went first, and she hit her first pitch way, way out into the outfield, which was awesome—but it only made me more nervous.

All I could think about was when my turn would be next. I was so distracted that I missed an easy pop-up that one girl hit right to me.

And then, before I knew it, I was standing at home plate, a bat in my hand. Coach Kendall was pitching, and Maggie, Sophie, and another girl were on the bases. My hands were shaking, and I felt like I was going to toss my Grainy Flakes all over the field.

"You can do it, Katie!" Alexis called out, and my mind flashed back to our practice session.

Think, I said. *You know what to do. Bend your knees. Don't hold the bat too high. Don't swing too early.*

But when Coach Kendall's first pitch came speeding toward me, I was so scared that I swung before it was even halfway to the plate.

"Just relax, Katie," Coach Adani said behind me. I took a deep breath and tried to focus. When the next pitch came, I forced myself to hold off swinging. Then I swung wildly.

"Foul ball!" Coach Adani called out as the ball veered off sharply to the right. At least I hadn't struck out.

I did strike out on the next turn, though. And then I hit two more fouls before I managed to get one near first base. I ran like crazy, and the only reason I was safe was because poor Maggie dropped the ball three times as she tried to pick it up.

It's over, I thought, my heart pounding. *For better or worse, it's over.*

After all the girls had a turn, Coach Kendall

had us all gather in a circle. "We'll put the team list in the front hall on Monday morning," she told us. "Those of you who don't make the team will be put on our alternate list. But no matter what happens, you should all be proud of how you performed today."

"Thank goodness that's over," I said out loud as the coaches walked away.

"I know, I was so nervous," said a voice behind me. It was Maggie.

"Me too," I agreed. "I almost threw up my breakfast."

Maggie laughed, and we started walking off the field together.

"So, I guess none of your friends are trying out?" I asked, hoping desperately that I would not end up on a team with Sydney.

Maggie shook her head. "Sydney's trying out for cheerleading," she answered. "So is Callie. And Bella is on the swim team."

"How come you're not trying out for cheerleading?" I asked. I thought Maggie did everything that Sydney did.

Maggie looked embarrassed for a second. "I could never do a cartwheel, no matter how hard I tried," she admitted. "Plus, I kind of want to do my own thing, you know? I really like softball. It's fun."

I suddenly realized that talking with Maggie wasn't so bad once she wasn't with the PGC—or making fun of me in gym. But then I heard Sydney's voice.

"Mags! Over here!"

Sydney walked up with Callie and Bella. "Maggie, oh my gosh, you are soooo sweaty!" she said, wrinkling her nose. (Of course, Sydney looked like she just stepped out of a makeup chair on a movie set.) "And, ew, gross, is that grass on your pants?"

Maggie looked flustered. Instead of answering Sydney, she started trying to rub off the grass stain.

"Yeah, you should have seen her," I said. "She dove to make this amazing catch."

Sydney looked at me like she had just noticed I existed.

"And what did you do?" she asked. "Accidentally throw the bat instead of the ball? Or maybe you knocked out the catcher with your silly arms."

Now it was my turn to clam up. I don't know why, but somehow it was easier to stick up for

Maggie than to stand up for myself. Besides, what could I say that would make any difference?

Maggie didn't tell Sydney that I didn't stink at softball, and I couldn't blame her. But I could blame Callie, who just stood there like she did last time and let Sydney be mean to me.

"Come on," Sydney said, nodding to her friends. "We need to get to that sale at Icon. But, Maggie, you definitely need a shower first. And please do not get any gross dirt in my mom's car!"

I really don't get Sydney sometimes. How can someone who looked so pretty and so sweet be so mean? Was she born that way? Did she squirt milk from her baby bottle at the other babies in the hospital? It's a mystery.

"Good luck, Katie," Callie said as she walked away. She said it kind of soft, and it didn't seem like Sydney heard her. She turned back around fast and just then Emma and Alexis ran up to me.

"You did great, Katie!" Emma said.

"I kept a record of how everyone did when they tried out," Alexis said. "I think you're in the top thirty or forty percent."

"So, does that mean I didn't totally stink out there?" I asked.

"Exactly," she answered. "It also means you're

94

probably good enough to make the team."

"I hope you're right," I said. But now that I was close, I had another reason to get nervous.

If I made the team, I'd actually have to play softball games. In front of people. With rules and winners and losers.

I grabbed my stomach and groaned. "I should never have eaten those Grainy Flakes."

CHAPTER 13

I'm Happy! . . . I Think

So did you have fun at tryouts?" Mom asked as she drove me home.

"Are you kidding? I was so nervous!" I said. "It was fearful, frightening, ferocious, and freaky—but definitely not fun. Why, are they supposed to be?"

"I guess not," Mom said, and she sounded a little worried.

As we drove through town I remembered something that took my mind off of the tryouts.

"Can we make a quick stop at Food City, please?" I asked. "I need to get some blueberries for the cupcakes."

Remember that blueberry frosting? I was going to ask Mom about it, but then I looked online to get some ideas. And I thought I had a way to make the perfect icing.

"Do you think you can help me try out this icing?" I asked Mom when we got home with the blueberries.

"Sure," Mom replied. "But why don't you take a shower first?"

"Good idea," I agreed. "I don't think sweaty cupcakes would taste so good."

A few minutes later I was squeaky clean, and Mom and I were setting up the food processor to begin my icing experiment. First I made a basic buttercream icing with butter, sugar, and vanilla. Normally we add a little bit of milk to make it creamy, but I wanted to hold off on that until I added the blueberries. I didn't want the icing to get too runny.

Then I put the blueberries in the food processor and with Mom's help we pureed them until they were supermushy. Then I put a strainer over the bowl and poured them into the strainer. The blueberry juice went into the bowl and the skins and seeds and stuff stayed in the strainer.

Next I poured the blueberry juice into the icing, a little at a time, and beat it in. It was a pretty, light purpley-blue color. But we were going for robin's-egg blue. So I added a couple of drops of gel color, and the blue became bright and happy—just like a robin's egg.

"What do you think?" I asked Mom.

"I think it's a lovely color," Mom said. "And I also think we need some cupcakes to go with it!"

I thought making cupcakes with my mom would take my mind off of softball, but when I was making the batter, it hit me.

I was making cupcake *batter*—and I was a terrible softball batter. Why could I be good at making batter but not actually be a good batter?

"Batter up!" I said, pouring the cupcakes into the tin, and Mom laughed.

And so I thought about the tryouts for the rest of the weekend. The only thing that cleared my mind was going on a run with Mom.

Monday morning I got on the bus and sat with Mia, like I always do.

"Sorry I missed your tryouts," Mia said. "How did it go?"

"Okay, I think," I said. "Alexis did her magical calculations, and she thinks I'll get in."

"You don't sound happy about that," Mia said, noticing the nervousness in my voice.

"I'm not sure how I feel," I confessed. "If I don't make the team, I'll feel like a loser. Plus, I'll disappoint everybody. But if I make the team, that means I'll have to play in games and that makes me nervous."

Mia nodded. "I get nervous sometimes before a game. But usually it goes away when I start playing."

Then she noticed the cupcake box in my hand. "What's that? It's not Friday."

I opened the lid a little bit. "I tried to get that blueberry icing right. What do you think?"

"It's so pretty!" Mia cried. She reached into her backpack and pulled out a sketchpad. "I did some designs over the weekend."

Mia showed me a sketch in colored pencils of a cupcake cake. On the bottom round layer, the cupcakes had green icing with flowers in pretty spring colors on them. The top two layers of cupcakes had blue icing and little birds on them. It looked absolutely beautiful.

"Oh, Mia, that's perfect!" I cried. "We can leave the blueberries out of the bottom ones and just use green food coloring."

"I found tiny cookie cutters shaped like flowers and birds," Mia said. "We can get different colors of fondant and roll it out and then cut out the shapes."

"Grandma Carole is going to love these cupcakes," I said.

George looked over the back of our seat. "Did somebody say cupcakes?" he said, eyeing the box.

"Sorry, George, these are for my friends," I said.

He made a sad face. "Aw, come on. I'm your friend, aren't I?"

I giggled. "Forget it, George!"

Then the bus pulled up in front of the school, and I started to feel nervous all over again.

"Come on," Mia said. "I'll go with you."

We walked up to the bulletin board in the front hall, and there it was: SOFTBALL TRYOUTS RESULTS. I took a deep breath and stared closer.

The list was alphabetical, so I saw my name right at the top: KATIE BROWN. I couldn't believe that I made it!

"Oh my gosh! I made it!" I said.

"I knew you would, Katie!" Mia said happily, and she gave me a hug.

I scanned the rest of the list and saw that Beth, Lucy, and Sophie had made the team, but Maggie was listed as an alternate. I felt kind of bad for her. I knew how much she wanted to play.

Then the opening bell rang, and I had to run to homeroom. I was dying to text Grandma Carole, but there's no texting allowed in our school.

When I got to the cafeteria later, I saw that Alexis and Emma were at the table already with Mia, instead of in the lunch line. They were all smiling.

"Congratulations!" they cried, and Alexis took her hands out from behind her back and presented me with an open cardboard box with four cupcakes inside. Each one was decorated to look like a softball.

"Thank you!" I cried. "These are so awesome. You didn't have to do that!"

"It's exciting," Alexis said. "Plus, I wanted to test out my cupcake idea."

"But what if I didn't get on the team?" I asked, teasing.

Emma held out another box of cupcakes. These said, "World's Best Friend" on top.

"Alexis had a backup plan," Emma admitted.

"Of course I did," Alexis said.

I held out my cupcake box. "Well, I brought

cupcakes too," I said. "I did a blueberry icing test."

"How are we possibly going to eat all these cupcakes?" Mia wondered aloud.

I had an idea. "I'm going to give one to George."

I picked up one of the blueberry cupcakes and walked across the cafeteria to George's table. On the way I passed the PGC table. Sydney was talking very loudly to Maggie.

"I don't understand why you're upset, Maggie. You're lucky you didn't make the team," Sydney was saying. "Why would you want to wear those ugly uniforms and get all dirty and sweaty just to play that boring game?"

Maggie looked like she might cry. "I—I just like it, that's all," she stammered.

Then Callie spoke up. "Leave her alone, Sydney. Maggie wanted to be on that team really bad."

Well, it's nice that she's standing up for Maggie, I thought as I walked past. *It would be even nicer if she would stick up for me once in a while.*

When I reached George's table, I put down the cupcake in front of him.

"You looked so pitiful before," I teased him.

"Thanks, Katie," George said. "I promise never to call you Silly Arms again."

If I had known that all I had to do was bribe George with cupcakes, I would have done that a long time ago.

"I hope you remember that," I said to George.

Then I walked back to my table, where my friends were waiting to celebrate with me.

CHAPTER 14

Can I Actually Do This?

So practice started on Monday after school and lasted until six thirty. By the time Mom picked me up I was sweaty, starving, and exhausted. And I still had to do my homework!

I have to say that I didn't do too badly in practice. But I still couldn't stop worrying. Every time I was in the field, I kept worrying that I would drop the ball or make a bad throw. And every time I was at bat, all I could think about was striking out. Which I did, a few times, but I got a few hits, too.

I think Coach Kendall knew I was nervous. Whenever I got up to bat, she would say, "Relax, Katie! Just have fun!"

Grandma Carole said the same thing when I called to tell her I made the team.

"You'll do great, Katie! Just have fun!"

Even my Cupcake Club friends had the same idea. One day at lunch, Mia asked me how practice was going.

"It's hard," I said. "And I keep worrying that I'm going to mess up."

"Just have fun," Alexis said. "Like we did when we had batting practice with Matt."

I thought about it. Practicing with Alexis and Matt had been kind of fun. But that's because they're my friends, and it didn't matter if I did good or not.

"I'll try," I said, but I knew I was kidding myself. I mean, how can you "just have fun" if something isn't fun?

Which is exactly what I asked my mom. "Everybody says 'just have fun,'" I said. "But how do I do that? It's not like I can turn on a switch in my brain or anything."

"I think everyone means to just relax and not take it so seriously," Mom said. "It's important to do your best, but in the end, it's just a game."

What Mom said made sense, but it didn't change anything. I still couldn't shut my brain off whenever I was at practice.

I did notice that one person was having a

lot of fun—Maggie. Even though she was an alternate, she came to every practice. Usually she was the first one to arrive. She asked to play different positions, too. One day she was in the outfield, the next day she'd be playing first base or at shortstop.

"You never know when coach will need me to play," Maggie told me. "And I want to be ready."

Maggie messed up a lot on the field, but she didn't let it get her down. She even made friends with the girls on the team really fast. I still didn't know some of their names.

One Tuesday we got our game schedule, and I saw that my first game was just four days away, on Saturday morning. We were playing the team from Fieldstone at their school field.

"Are you sure the game is *this* Saturday?" I asked Coach Kendall. "I mean, we're not actually ready to play another team, are we?"

"Playing another team is the best way to get experience," Coach Kendall said. "And a lot of their players are new, just like you. It'll be fine."

The Friday night before the game I didn't sleep very well. I dreamed that I kept swinging and swinging and striking out, and everyone in the stands was pointing and laughing at me.

The game the next morning was at eleven, but once again I woke up superearly. Thankfully, Mom woke up early too, and we went for a run. The sound of the chirping birds and the gentle breeze blowing through the trees in the park all helped to calm me down a little bit.

When I got home I changed into my softball uniform: gold baseball pants, white socks, black cleats, and a blue shirt that said PARK STREET MIDDLE SCHOOL in gold letters. I put my hair in a low ponytail, so I could fit my hat over it.

I looked at my reflection in the mirror. I looked just like a real softball player.

"This is it, Katie," I whispered to myself.

Even though the game started at eleven, Mom dropped me off at ten, so I could warm up with the team.

"I'll be back later," she promised. "And Katie—"

"Please don't say, 'just have fun,'" I said.

Mom smiled. "I was going to say, just do your best and you won't have anything to worry about."

"Thanks, Mom," I said.

I got out of the car and ran toward my team. On the other side of the field, the Fieldstone girls in their black and gray uniforms were warming up. It might have been my imagination, but I swear they all looked bigger and stronger than all of us.

To warm up, we did some exercises and then practiced throwing and catching. The whole time my head felt like it was full of cotton balls—so full of fear that I pretty much drowned out everything all around me. It was a really weird feeling.

We were walking to our dugout when a loud cheer erupted from the stands, and I looked up. Alexis, Emma, and Mia were holding up a big sign that said, GO, KATIE! Mom was sitting next to Mia, and sitting next to Mom was a lady with white hair, wearing a blue T-shirt and a gold baseball cap.

I couldn't believe it. "Grandma?"

Grandma Carole saw me looking and started waving like crazy. "Surprise, Katie-kins!" she yelled.

I felt like everybody was looking at me, which was embarrassing, but I was still happy to see Grandma. I ran over to the stands, and she climbed down to meet me by the fence.

"I came a week early to surprise you," she said.

"I can't believe it!" I said.

Grandma grinned. "I wouldn't miss this for anything. Go get 'em, Katie-kins!"

I was really happy that Grandma was here, but now I really didn't want to mess up. I gulped hard and ran back to the field.

CHAPTER 15

Are You Sure Those Other Players Aren't Professionals?

It felt good to have my own personal cheering section, but I also felt like it was extra pressure, too. Like everybody would be watching my every move.

They must be wondering, Who is this Katie? I thought. *She must be pretty awesome to have people here holding up such a big sign for her.*

So the game started, and I learned that when you're playing at another field, they have to let you go first. Which meant we were up at bat first.

Luckily, Coach Kendall had me batting sixth.

Maybe I won't have to bat this inning, I thought. *Maybe everybody else will strike out.*

As soon as I had the thought, I felt terrible. Of course I didn't want anyone to strike out. I wanted us to win. Right? Of course I did. Winning was the goal here, wasn't it? Or was it just to have fun, like Mom and everyone kept telling me?

Tanya, the girl who batted first, struck out. I felt really guilty that my first thought was "Good, at least someone else struck out before me." But then Beth got up, and she hit a grounder to left field and made it to first base. Sophie was up next, and she walked, so there was someone on first and second. Then on Lucy's turn she hit a ball way into the outfield. It bounced once, but the fielder got it fast and threw it back to the pitcher, so Beth couldn't make it home and was stuck on third base.

The bases were loaded. My palms were starting to sweat like crazy, and Sam wasn't even around. I held my breath when a girl named Sarah went to bat. She ended up striking out, too.

It was the first inning of my first game, and it was bases loaded with two players out. If you're a superstar hitter, this is your dream situation. But if you're a not so great hitter, like me, it's pretty much your worst nightmare. So you can imagine how I felt.

The fuzziness in my head was worse than ever, and I swear I could have filled a gallon milk jug with all the sweat from my palms. I was so frozen with fear that when the first pitch came at me, I didn't even swing. Unfortunately, it was a perfect pitch.

"Strike!" the umpire called out.

Swing, I willed myself. *Just swing next time!*

So when the next ball came, I swung—way too early, like I do when I'm not focused.

"Strike two!"

When the third ball whizzed at me, I tried to stay focused. But I should have wiped my sweaty palms on my pants, because even though I swung on time, the bat slipped a little in my hands, and I missed the ball.

"Strike three!"

The other team started running off the field, and I was confused for a second until I realized the half was over. We had lost our chance to score, all because of me.

"Good job, girls!" Coach Kendall called out. "Now let's get out there!"

I was still standing at home plate, kind of dazed. "It's okay, Katie!" I heard, and I looked behind me. It was Maggie. "Just shake it off!" Was Maggie pulling a Ms. Chen, telling me to just shake it off? "You're doing great, Katie!" yelled Maggie. Wow, was Maggie actually being nice to me? I was so surprised that I kept standing there.

"C'mon, Katie!" called Coach Kendall.

I put down the bat and helmet, grabbed my glove, and jogged over to my position on second base. I quickly glanced at the stands, where Mom, Grandma, and my friends were still smiling and cheering. Didn't they just see me strike out?

Sarah, the girl who had struck out before me, was pitching. I braced myself as the first Fieldstone batter came up to home plate. She looked about six feet tall and had muscles like a bodybuilder. Okay, maybe that's not exactly true, but that's how she looked in my mind. I was convinced we were playing a team of professionals in disguise.

The Fieldstone batter made contact on the first pitch, whacking the ball way into the outfield. Tanya was out there, and she missed the ball, but Sophie ran and scooped it up. I saw the batter touch first base and figured that was the end of the play.

Then I heard Sophie cry out, "Katie! Katie!"

I turned and saw her throwing the ball to me. To my horror the batter was making her way to second!

My heart was in my throat as I quickly got under the ball and caught it. For a second I stood there, frozen.

"Katie, tag the runner!" Coach Kendall called out.

I had forgotten all about that part. I ran to the Fieldstone player as fast as I could and touched her with my glove about a second before she got to the base.

"Out!" the umpire called, and I almost fainted with relief. Everyone in the stands cheered. Out of the corner of my eye I saw Grandma jump up. Oh boy, I really hope she wasn't yelling "Yay, Katie-kins!" That would be harder to live down than Silly Arms.

I tried to concentrate. Almost messing up the play really bothered me. I kept thinking about it over and over, and so when the next batter hit an easy pop-up, I let it bounce out of my glove. The rest of the inning was brutal. Each Fieldstone batter was stronger than the next, and by the time the inning ended, they had scored two runs.

Lucy tried to psych us up as we ran back to the dugout for the next inning. "It's just the first inning!" she said. "We can come back strong!"

But the game was a total disaster. Every time I was at bat I either fouled out or struck out, and lots of other girls were striking out too. The more runs the other team scored, the worse we played.

We had a chance in the third inning to score some runs. We had a runner on third base. There were two outs. Lucy was up.

"Go get 'em, Lucy!" I cheered. But then the catcher called time out and went to the mound to speak to the pitcher. The pitcher nodded, and the catcher trotted back to her position behind the plate. Then the catcher held her right arm straight out. The pitcher threw the ball to her right hand, far away so the batter couldn't swing. She did this four times; it was an intentional walk. Lucy trotted out to first base.

At first I didn't understand why the pitcher would intentionally want to put another batter on base. And then I understood. They intentionally walked Lucy to get to me because they figured I would be an easy out. Wow, these girls were just as bad as Sydney! Why would they be that mean? I knew it was about winning, but boy that made me even more determined than ever to get a hit. But I was overeager and swung at everything. Three quick strikes, and I was done.

The Fieldstone team didn't even need to go up to bat in the seventh inning, because they had already won the game: 12–2.

We didn't just lose—we lost badly. But I didn't

mind losing as much as I minded how badly I had played. Mom told me to do my best. If that was my best, I was in trouble.

Coach Kendall gave us a pep talk in the dugout. "This was a good first effort, girls," she said. "We're still learning how to play together as a team. You'll see—we'll do better each time we play."

"When's our next game?" someone asked.

"Monday night," Coach Kendall said. "We'll meet an hour early, so we can practice beforehand."

Another game in two days? My stomach hurt just thinking about it. And every time I thought about the pitcher walking Lucy to get to me, my face burned.

But something else was upsetting me even more. Grandma Carole had come out early just to see me play. She had so much confidence in me and was sure I would do well. I felt like I had let her down. She must be so disappointed in me. How could I face her now?

Maggie was trying to cheer everyone up. *Maybe she should have tried out for cheerleading after all,* I thought grumpily.

"Hey, Katie, nice work!" she said. "You really went down swinging!"

I tensed up. Was she making fun of me?

But when I looked at her she looked friendly. "You weren't going down without a fight!" she said.

"Thanks," I mumbled.

Maggie hadn't even played in the game. Maybe that's why she didn't feel so badly. None of the strikeouts were her fault.

"See you on Monday!" she said with a wave.

"See you," I said. Then I turned to face the stands, where my fan club was waiting for me.

CHAPTER 16

I Learn Something New About Grandma

After Coach Kendall finished her speech, I slowly walked to the stands. Mom, Grandma, and my friends were all coming toward me, smiling.

"It's all right, it's okay, you did a great job, anyway!" Mom cheered, and at that moment I wished the ground would open and swallow me up.

"Well, I wouldn't say 'great,' exactly," I told her.

Grandma put her arm around me. "It's just first-game jitters, that's all," she said. "I'm sure you'll do great at your next game."

My next game. The thought made my stomach flip-flop again.

Mom turned to the Cupcake Club. "Can you girls join us for some pizza?"

Vinnie's Pizza was just a few blocks from the

field, so we walked there. We couldn't have all fit in the car, anyway. Mom and Grandma walked ahead of us. Thankfully, we started talking about cupcakes instead of going over that disaster of a game.

"You know, now that your grandma is here early, it will be hard to surprise her with a cupcake cake," Alexis pointed out.

"I didn't think of that," I admitted. "The party's Friday night, so we should bake on Thursday."

"We can probably do it at my house," Mia offered.

"Cool," I said. Then I remembered something. "Mia, aren't you with your dad next weekend?" It made me sad to think she would miss the party.

"Dad said I could come out Saturday morning instead," Mia said with a grin. "So I can bring the cupcake cake with me Friday night."

"Double cool," I said.

We found a big table in the pizza parlor, and Mom ordered one plain pie and one pie loaded with veggies, Grandma's favorite. The pizza was delicious, and of course we ended up talking about softball.

Grandma held up her glass of water. "Cheers to Katie! I'm so proud of you for playing your first game."

Everyone clinked their glasses together.

"I was so nervous," I admitted. "I couldn't focus. And besides, we lost—in a major way."

"You can't win all the time," Alexis said. "Our soccer team lost our last three games. That's just how it is sometimes."

"But don't you get nervous when you play?" I asked.

Alexis shrugged. "Not really. I just play."

I saw Mom and Grandma look at each other. Then Mom got up to pay the bill. Grandma smiled at us.

"I heard you girls are making a cupcake cake for my party," she said. "I can't wait to see it. Maybe you can give me just a little hint about it?"

I shook my head. "Sorry, Grandma. We want it to be a surprise."

"One hint is that it will be delicious!" Mia said.

"Oh, I'm sure it will!" said Grandma.

"Katie told us you used to bake professionally," said Alexis.

"Yes," Grandma said. "But that was a long time ago. And now I'm happy you girls are baking for me. I like eating cupcakes more than I like baking them!"

We left Vinnie's and walked back to the field. Grandma Carole pointed to the grassy lawn, where a gray bird with a black head and a red belly was hopping on the ground.

"There it is! The first robin of spring!" she said. She looked at me. "It always brings me good luck. And I think it's extra lucky that I saw it with you."

Grandma walked ahead, and I looked at the Cupcake Club and smiled. We had definitely designed the perfect cupcake cake for her!

But when we got back home, I wasn't smiling anymore. I kept thinking about Monday's game.

"Katie, come sit down at the kitchen table with us," Mom said.

Uh-oh, I thought. *I must be in trouble for something.* Maybe they were going to tell me all the things I did wrong in the game.

But Mom asked me something I wasn't expecting. "Katie, Grandma Carole and I have noticed that you are not yourself today. Is something bothering you?"

"Well, I guess . . ." I didn't want to disappoint them.

"It's okay, Katie," Grandma Carole said. "We're here to help."

I took a deep breath. "It's like this," I said. "I know I'm okay at softball. And I like playing catch with my friends and even having batting practice

121

with Matt. But being on the team . . . it's so much pressure. I'm not having any fun at all."

"I understand," Grandma Carole said, nodding, and I was kind of surprised.

"You do?" I asked, surprised.

"I do. There's a reason I quit baking professionally," she said. "I love to bake, but once I started doing it as a business, it wasn't fun anymore. I felt all this pressure to make things perfect. One day I was making a cake and I realized that I was hating what I was doing. That's when I knew I had to stop and end the business."

"That's exactly how I feel about softball," I said.

"I figured that because I recognized the look on your face," Grandma said. "I'm sorry if I pushed you into sports at all."

"You didn't, Grandma," I said honestly. "I wanted to try. It wasn't just about making a team. I just don't want to stink at sports anymore. I don't want to be the worst kid at everything in gym class."

"You can be athletic without being on a team," Mom pointed out. "You can still play with your friends for fun. And I'll throw a ball around with you whenever you want."

"And I won't make you play tennis anymore," Grandma said with a grin. "The important thing,

Katie, is that you do things that are good for you and make you happy."

I grinned back. "I just remembered something. There is one sport that I'm good at, and I don't ever need to be on a team. And the two of you are really good at it too."

Mom and Grandma looked at each other, confused.

"Running! Anybody want to go for a run?" I asked.

Mom and Grandma both stood up.

"You bet!" Grandma Carole said. "Let me go get changed."

A few minutes later the three of us were jogging through the park, under the trees.

And I didn't feel nervous at all! In fact, I felt great.

Sydney

me!

CHAPTER 17

My Moment in Gym Class

When I woke up Monday I knew what I had to do, and it wasn't going to be easy. Instead of taking the bus, I asked Mom to drop me off at school a few minutes early. I had practiced what I was going to say with her. "Take a big breath," she said as I opened the car door. "It will be fine."

"I know," I lied.

"I love you, sweetie!" she called out, and I waved and shut the door fast. I love my mom, but you do not want your mom yelling "I love you" in front of the entire middle school, for goodness's sake.

I took a deep breath. Then I went and found Coach Kendall in the gym office.

I knocked on the door. "Coach Kendall?"

"Oh, hi, Katie," she said, looking up at me. "Come on in."

I sat in the metal chair on the other side of her desk. Then I took another deep breath.

"So, I think I need to quit the team," I blurted out. That is not how I planned to say it, but it just came out.

"Is everything okay?" the coach asked.

"Yeah, I'm fine, except that I just get too nervous when I'm playing," I said. "Everybody says to relax and have fun, but I can't."

"But you've just started, and you've got talent, Katie," Coach Kendall said. "I'm sure you'll feel more confident the more you play."

I shook my head. "I don't think so. It's a lot of pressure. I just don't think I can do it. I like playing in the backyard with my friends, but I really hated playing during the game. I got nervous, and I didn't sleep the night before the game. And, honestly, I just kind of hated every minute of it. And I know we just had one game, but I thought about it all weekend, and I don't think softball is for me. Honestly, I almost threw up thinking about playing a game tonight. I'm sorry. I hope I didn't disappoint you."

Whew, well, at least I finally got out what I practiced with Mom.

Coach Kendall frowned a little and nodded her head. "Competitive sports aren't for everybody. I certainly don't want you to be unhappy. But if you change your mind and feel like trying out next year, I'd be happy to have you on the team."

"Thanks," I said. "And thanks for understanding."

Then I left the gym, and even though I felt kind of bad about quitting, I also felt like a big rock had been taken off my shoulders. Like I could float or fly. What a relief!

Now I just had to tell my friends.

At lunch I waited until Alexis and Emma sat down with me and Mia. Then I just spit it out (not my lunch, my news).

"So I quit the softball team this morning," I blurted out.

"Oh no!" Emma said. "But you tried so hard."

"I know," I said. "But I can't take the pressure. I was miserable. I like playing for fun. But for real in a game, it's not for me."

Mia nodded. "Yeah, you looked pretty miserable on Saturday. Like all of your Katie energy was sucked right out of you."

That's why Mia is my new best friend. She totally gets me.

"Exactly," I said. "Anyway, thanks for helping me

out so much, you guys. And I'll still play ball with you and stuff. I just don't want to be on a team."

"So does this mean you're not going to find another after-school activity?" Alexis asked.

"Well, I have one new activity. I am running now," I said. "I go with my mom or grandmother. I really love it. I just put my sneakers on and go, and there's no pressure or anything. And I feel great afterward."

"Hey, you should try out for the track team!" said Alexis.

"I don't think so," I said. "That's the thing about running. It's just me and my legs taking me along. I'm not worried about teammates or letting anyone down or who is watching me. It feels great to just run."

"We do track as a unit in gym," said Emma. "Just think about how great you'll be!"

"And we have softball, too," said Mia. "So that's a bunch of gym classes you should ace!"

"I hadn't thought about that," I said. But it was true. Some worry-free gym classes wouldn't be too bad.

A lot of surprising things had happened in the last few weeks. I had made the softball team. I learned that Grandma Carole and I were more alike than I thought. And then another surprising thing happened, right there at lunch.

Maggie walked up to me as I went to throw out my garbage—and she wasn't following Sydney or the other PGC girls.

"I heard you quit the team," she said. "Why? You were good."

I nodded. "It's kind of hard to explain, but mostly I just wasn't having fun."

Maggie shook her head. "Are you serious? Because I think it's really fun," she said.

I felt my neck get stiff. "Well it wasn't for me," I said a little defensively.

"My mom says there's enough stuff you have to do that you don't like, and that when you can choose, you should always choose the things you love," said Maggie. "So I get that."

I smiled. "Thanks," I said. Maybe I should be giving Maggie more of a break. What she just said sounded like something my mom would say.

"Anyway, I came to thank you. Coach Kendall gave me your spot on the team. I'm so excited. I'm sorry you didn't like it, but I'm hoping I'll be able to catch as well as you."

I was happy then. Maggie deserved it.

Then she leaned close to me. "And I don't care

what Sydney thinks!" she whispered.

I laughed as Maggie walked away. Alexis raised an eyebrow.

"What was that all about?" she asked.

"Maggie's on the team now," I said. "I'm happy for her."

"But doesn't she torture you in gym?" Emma asked.

I shrugged. "Sometimes. But she's not so bad, especially when she's away from Sydney."

That reminded me of my only lasting problem: Sydney. More exactly, Sydney in gym class. We had been playing flag football for a few weeks, and I hadn't gotten any better. Although ever since I gave George that cupcake, he had kept his promise and stopped calling me Silly Arms.

"If only we were done with flag football," I said with a sigh. "I guess I am doomed to be a flag-football spaz forever."

"I'm sorry," Emma said. "But lately Sydney seems more interested in bumping into the boys than bothering you, anyway."

"Good point," I agreed. "Maybe I can practice turning invisible in gym. I heard if you concentrate long enough, it can happen."

"That can't be true," Alexis said.

"Of course not, but I can try," I said.

When I got to gym class later, Ms. Chen had an announcement to make after we did our warm-up exercises.

"The state physical fitness tests are next month," she said. "We're going to start training today. Let's start with some running. Ten times around the gym. Let's move it!"

I can handle that, I thought with relief. Maybe my worry-free gym class was starting sooner than I thought. But as soon as I started running, Sydney started in on me.

"Be careful, Katie, or you'll trip over your own feet!" she said. Then her voice got louder. "Hey, everybody, watch out for Katie! She might crash into you." She smirked and tossed her long, perfect, shiny hair.

This time Sydney's teasing didn't bother me much—maybe because I knew how wrong she was.

"I think I'll be just fine," I told her, and then I ran right past her. I pretended I was in the park with the birds and started flying around the gym, getting ahead of everybody—even the boys.

"Nice hustle, Katie!" Ms. Chen called out. "Sydney, look alive out there! This isn't a funeral march!"

I looked back and saw that Sydney was one of the last runners, and she actually looked a little bit sweaty. I smiled.

"Go, Silly Legs!" called George. "The girl can run!" *I have to start bringing him more cupcakes,* I thought, and sprinted toward the finish.

In a couple of months we'd be playing basketball or volleyball or whatever, and I'd be back to being a spaz again. But for now, all I had to do was run.

CHAPTER 18

I Don't Mean to Brag, but I Am Pretty Talented After All!

The rest of the week went by very fast. It was nice having Grandma Carole there early, because I didn't have to go to Mom's office after school. She helped me with my homework, and we made dinner together.

Then Thursday was pretty crazy. After school I met Alexis and Emma at Mia's house, and we started on the cupcake cake. Mia's mom was nice and got us Chinese food to eat while the cupcakes cooled down. Then we decorated them with fondant flowers, leaves, and birds in shades of yellow, pink, green, violet, and blue. When we were all done, we boxed them up. Tomorrow, at the party, we would put them on their stands.

Mom picked me up at eight thirty. She had been

decorating the house while we made the cupcakes. Grandma was staying at Uncle Jimmy's tonight. "Everything looks great," she said. "Barbara helped me set it all up. It looks so beautiful."

Barbara is Callie's mom. I knew Callie and her family would be at the party tomorrow, and I wasn't sure how I felt about it. I was still pretty mad at Callie for not sticking up for me.

But I didn't tell my mom that. "I can't wait to see it," I said.

Mom was right about the decorations. The whole house looked like a spring garden, with light green tablecloths and a pretty flower arrangement on each table. The streamers on the ceiling were green and yellow and robin's-egg blue, a perfect match for our cupcake cake.

The next day we got up really early. Mia and her stepdad arrived not long after. Eddie was carrying the cupcake boxes, and Mia had the stands.

"Over there," Mom instructed, pointing to a little round table in a corner of the room. "I can't wait to see them!"

Emma and Alexis arrived next, so all four of us were able to set up the cupcake cake. We started with the green flower cupcakes on the bottom, and the top two tiers were blue with birds on them, just like in Mia's drawing.

"Oh, it's absolutely beautiful!"

Grandma Carole walked in, wearing a blue dress that almost matched the cupcakes. Grandpa Chuck was there too, and he wore a robin's-egg-blue tie with his gray suit.

Grandma walked around the cupcake table, admiring it from every angle.

"This is absolutely perfect!" she cried. "Robin's-egg blue! I love it!"

"And the cupcakes are blueberry, too," I said.

"My favorite!" Grandma said. "You girls are very talented. Your business must be doing very well."

"Our profits are rising every month," Alexis reported proudly.

Then the party guests started streaming in, and Joanne from Mom's office started playing songs from her iPod on a speaker. It really felt like a party.

Then Callie came in with her older sister, Jenna, and her mom and dad. Mr. Wilson gave me a big hug when he saw me.

"Hey there, Katie-did," he said. "My gosh, you must have grown a foot since I last saw you!"

"Not a foot," I said. "But maybe a little."

Then Callie's parents walked off to say hi to my

grandparents, and Callie and I were just standing there, looking at each other. Callie looked kind of embarrassed.

"So, I just wanted to say that I felt kind of bad about the way Sydney's been talking to you," she said. "I wanted to stick up for you, but Sydney . . ."

"It's okay," I said, thinking of gym the other day. "I can take care of myself. Besides, I don't really care what Sydney thinks, anyway."

I didn't believe it until I said it out loud, but it was true. Sydney could say whatever she wanted, but as long as it didn't matter to me, it couldn't hurt me, right?

Callie looked a little surprised. "Um, that's cool, then."

That's when Mia ran up and grabbed me by the arm. "Katie, I looooove this song. Let's dance!"

We all danced and ate a bunch of food, and Mom showed a slideshow of photos of Grandma from when she was a little girl.

"Wow, Katie, you look just like your grandma," Emma remarked.

"I know," I said proudly.

Then Grandpa Chuck walked up to me. "Katie, I hear you're a fine softball player. How about a game outside?"

I hesitated, but then he said, "Just for fun. We won't even keep score."

Then I relaxed. "Sure," I said.

So some of us went outside and played softball for a while, and it *was* fun. And something amazing even happened. I hit a home run!

The ball went way into the outfield, and Alexis ran for it, but couldn't catch it. So I ran around the bases as fast as I could.

"Go, Katie-kins!" Grandma Carole cheered as I crossed home plate. My heart was pounding and I was very sweaty, but not because I was nervous—I was excited.

Finally it was time for cupcakes. After Grandma Carole blew out her candles, everyone dug in.

"Katie, these cupcakes are delicious!" Grandma said. "You could be a professional baker."

"We all made them," I said, blushing.

"Yes, but Katie figured out the frosting," Mia pointed out.

Mom hugged me. "You know what you're great at besides baking cupcakes?" she asked me.

"No, what?"

"You're a good friend," Mom said. "And a wonderful running partner."

"And a pretty good batter," Grandpa added.

"And the best granddaughter ever!" Grandma Carole said, joining me and Mom in a group hug.

I counted in my head—that was one, two, three, four, five talents! Not bad, don't you think? I smiled at everyone around me as they happily ate delicious cupcakes.

Then I remembered to save a cupcake for George. I'd need it—pretty soon in gym we'd be starting basketball!

Want another sweet cupcake?

Here's a sneak peek
of the sixth book in the

CUPCaKe  DIARIES

series:

Mia's

baker's dozen

I'll Definitely Finish It Tomorrow

Me llamo Mia y me gusta hornear pastelitos.

That means "My name is Mia, and I like to bake cupcakes" in Spanish. A few months ago, I could never have read that sentence or even written it. Maybe that doesn't sound like a big deal. But for me, it totally was.

Here's the thing: I'm good at a bunch of things, like playing soccer and drawing and decorating cupcakes. Nobody ever *expected* me to be good at them. I just was.

But everyone expected me to be good at Spanish. My whole family is Latino, and my mom and dad both speak Spanish. I've been hearing it since I was a baby, and I can understand a lot of it and speak it pretty well—enough to get my point across. But reading and writing Spanish? That's a whole other thing. And the fact that I was bad at it got me into a big mess.

The whole situation kind of blew up this winter. You see, when I started middle school in the fall, they placed me in Advanced Spanish with Señora Delgado. At first I did okay, but after a few weeks it was pretty clear to me that I was in over my head. The homework kept getting harder and harder, and my test grades were slipping.

One night in February, I was trying really hard to do my Spanish homework. Señora asked us to write an essay about something we planned to do this month. I decided to write about going to see my dad, who lives in Manhattan. I visit him every other weekend, and we always go out to eat sushi.

It sounds simple, but I was having a hard time. I always get mixed up with the verbs, and that was the whole point of the essay—to use future indicative verbs. (Yeah, I'm not sure what those are either.) Anyway, I was trying to write "We will eat sushi," and I couldn't get the verb right.

"Comemos"? Or is it "comeramos"? I wondered aloud with a frown while tapping my pencil on my desk. My head was starting to really hurt,

and it wasn't just because of the homework.

"Dan, TURN IT DOWN!" I yelled at the wall in front of me. On the other side, Dan, my stepbrother, was blasting music, like he always does. He listens to metal or something, and it sounds like a werewolf screaming in a thunderstorm. He couldn't hear me, so I started banging on the walls.

The music got a little bit softer, and Dan yelled, "Chill, Mia!"

"Thanks," I muttered, even though I knew he couldn't hear me.

I looked back down at my paper, which was only half finished. Where was I again? Oh, right. Sushi. At least that word is the same in any language.

My brain couldn't take any more. I picked up my smartphone and messaged three of my friends at once.

Anyone NOT want to do homework right now? I asked.

Alexis replied first. She's the fastest texter in the Cupcake Club.

Mine is already done!

Of course, I should have known. Alexis is one of those people who actually likes doing homework.

It's better than babysitting my little brother! came the next reply.

That's my friend Emma. I actually think her little brother Jake is kind of cute, but I also know that he can be annoying.

The last reply came from my friend Katie.

Let's go on a homework strike!

I laughed. Katie is really funny, and she also feels the same way I do about a lot of things (like homework). That's probably why she's my best friend here in Maple Grove.

Where are we meeting tomorrow? I asked.

I think I mentioned the Cupcake Club already. That's a business I started with Alexis, Emma, and Katie. We bake cupcakes for parties and other events, and we meet at least once a week.

We can do it at my house, Emma replied.
Works for me! Alexis texted back at light-speed.

She always likes going to Emma's house, and it's not just because she and Emma are best friends. She used to have a crush on Emma's brother Matt. He's pretty cute, but Emma's brother Sam is even cuter.

Alexis texted again.

Everyone come with ideas for the Valentine's cupcakes.

Ugh! I hate that holiday! Emma complained.
But there's CANDY! Katie wrote.
And everything's pink, I reminded Emma since pink is her favorite color.
K, you have a point. But still. We have to watch all the "couples" in school make a big deal out of it, Emma replied.
And watch all the boys go gaga for Sydney, Alexis chimed in.

Sydney is the president of the Popular Girls Club, and Alexis is right—lots of boys like her.

Any boys who like Sydney have cupcakes for brains, Katie wrote.

I laughed.

Got to go! Twelve more math problems left! Emma wrote.

I have 2 go study, Alexis added.

I thought you were done? Katie wrote.

This is just for fun ☺, Alexis wrote back.

If u want to have fun u can do my homework, Katie typed.

Or mine, I added.

LOL! CU tom, Alexis typed.

I said good night to my friends and put down my phone. I stared at my paper for a few seconds and then I picked up my sketchbook.

My Spanish class isn't until after lunch, so I figured I could finish the essay then. I couldn't concentrate now anyway. Besides, I was dying to finish a sketch I had started earlier.

My mom's a fashion stylist and she's always taking the train to New York to meet with designers and boutique owners. I guess I take after her because I am totally obsessed with fashion and I love designing my own clothes. Once in a while, Mom takes me to meetings with her and I get to see all the latest fashions before other people do.

Lately I've been trying to design a winter coat

that keeps you warm but isn't all puffy. I hate puffy coats.

I opened up my sketchbook, a new one that my dad gave me. It's got this soft leather cover and really good paper inside that makes my drawings look even better. I picked up a purple pencil and started to finish my sketch of a knee-length wrap-around style coat.

There was a knock on my door, and then Mom stepped in.

"Hey, sweetie," she said. She nodded to the sketchbook. "Done with your homework?"

"Yes," I lied.

Mom smiled and walked over to look at my sketch. "Very nice, *mija*," she said. "I like the shape of those sleeves."

"Thanks!" I replied, and she kissed me on the head and left the room. I started to feel a little guilty about lying about my homework, but I pushed the feeling aside. I was definitely going to finish it tomorrow, so no problem, right?

Actually, it was a problem . . . a big one.

Coco Simon always dreamed of opening a cupcake bakery but was afraid she would eat all of the profits. When she's not daydreaming about cupcakes, Coco edits children's books and has written close to one hundred books for children, tweens, and young adults, which is a lot less than the number of cupcakes she's eaten. Cupcake Diaries is the first time Coco has mixed her love of cupcakes with writing.

Still Hungry?

There's always room for another Cupcake!

Katie and the Cupcake Cure
978-1-4424-2275-9 $5.99
978-1-4424-2276-6 (eBook)

Mia in the Mix
978-1-4424-2277-3 $5.99
978-1-4424-2278-0 (eBook)

Emma on Thin Icing
978-1-4424-2279-7 $5.99
978-1-4424-2280-3 (eBook)

Alexis and the Perfect Recipe
978-1-4424-2901-7 $5.99
978-1-4424-2902-4 (eBook)

Katie, Batter Up!
978-1-4424-4611-3 $5.99
978-1-4424-4612-0 (eBook)

Mia's Baker's Dozen
978-1-4424-4613-7 $5.99
978-1-4424-4614-4 (eBook)

Emma All Stirred Up!
978-1-4424-5078-3 $5.99
978-1-4424-5079-0 (eBook)

Alexis Cool as a Cupcake
978-1-4424-5080-6 $5.99
978-1-4424-5081-3 (eBook)

Katie and the Cupcake War
978-1-4424-5373-9 $5.99
978-1-4424-5374-6 (eBook)

Mia's Boiling Point

978-1-4424-5396-8 $5.99
978-1-4424-5397-5 (eBook)

Emma, Smile and Say "Cupcake!"

978-1-4424-5398-2 $5.99
978-1-4424-5400-2 (eBook)

Alexis Gets Frosted

978-1-4424-6867-2 $5.99
978-1-4424-6868-9 (eBook)

Katie's New Recipe

978-1-4424-7168-9 $5.99
978-1-4424-7169-6 (eBook)

Mia a Matter of Taste

978-1-4424-7435-2 $5.99
978-1-4424-7436-9 (eBook)

Emma Sugar and Spice and Everything Nice
978-1-4424-7481-9 $5.99
978-1-4424-7489-5 (eBook)

Alexis and the Missing Ingredient
978-1-4424-8587-7 $5.99
978-1-4424-8589-1 (eBook)

Katie Sprinkles & Surprises
978-1-4424-8590-7 $5.99
978-1-4424-8592-1 (eBook)

Mia Fashion Plates and Cupcakes
978-1-4424-9790-0 $5.99
978-1-4424-9792-4 (eBook)